"Las Vegas," Evan read aloud as he passed yet another road sign. "Via 60 North." It took a minute for the words to sink in, but when they did, Evan's eyes lit up. Immediately he glanced at the number of miles on the sign and started doing the math. *That means we could be there by . . . seven-thirty.*

How could he ignore the karma that had put him behind the wheel at this crucial moment? The road was practically *calling* to him. And a slight detour wouldn't keep them from getting to Jeremy's family by tomorrow evening. He glanced over at Jeremy, who was still fast asleep, then over his shoulder at Conner.

"So what do you say, guys? Should we do Vegas?" Jeremy shifted slightly in his seat and mumbled something that sounded like, "Jessica." In the backseat Conner's mouth dropped open, and he began to snore.

"I'll take that as a yes," Evan said, a wide grin spreading across his face. He turned the wheel ever so slightly and took the exit. Las Vegas was exactly what Evan needed. And it was exactly what Conner and Jeremy needed, whether they wanted to admit it or not.

Don't miss any of the books in SWEET VALLEY HIGH
SENIOR YEAR, an exciting series from Bantam Books!

#1 CAN'T STAY AWAY
#2 SAY IT TO MY FACE
#3 SO COOL
#4 I'VE GOT A SECRET
#5 IF YOU ONLY KNEW
#6 YOUR BASIC NIGHTMARE
#7 BOY MEETS GIRL
#8 MARIA WHO?
#9 THE ONE THAT GOT AWAY
#10 BROKEN ANGEL
#11 TAKE ME ON
#12 BAD GIRL
#13 ALL ABOUT LOVE
#14 SPLIT DECISION
#15 ON MY OWN
#16 THREE GIRLS AND A GUY
#17 BACKSTABBER
#18 AS IF I CARE
#19 IT'S MY LIFE
#20 NOTHING IS FOREVER
#21 THE IT GUY
#22 SO NOT ME
#23 FALLING APART
#24 NEVER LET GO
#25 STRAIGHT UP
#26 TOO LATE
#27 PLAYING DIRTY
#28 MEANT TO BE
#29 WHERE WE BELONG
#30 CLOSE TO YOU
#31 STAY OR GO
#32 ROAD TRIP

Visit the Official Sweet Valley Web Site on the Internet at:

www.sweetvalley.com

Francine Pascal's SVH senioryear

Road Trip

CREATED BY
FRANCINE PASCAL

BANTAM BOOKS
NEW YORK · TORONTO · LONDON · SYDNEY · AUCKLAND

To Julia Miller

RL: 6, AGES 012 AND UP

ROAD TRIP
A Bantam Book / August 2001

Sweet Valley High® is a registered trademark of Francine Pascal.
Conceived by Francine Pascal.
Cover photography by Michael Segal.

Copyright © 2001 by Francine Pascal.
Cover copyright © 2001 by 17th Street Productions,
an Alloy Online, Inc. company.

Produced by 17th Street Productions,
an Alloy Online, Inc. company.
33 West 17th Street
New York, NY 10011.

ISBN: 0-553-49381-7

Visit us on the Web! www.randomhouse.com/teens

Published simultaneously in the United States and Canada

Bantam Books is an imprint of Random House Children's Books, a
division of Random House, Inc. BANTAM BOOKS and the rooster
colophon are registered trademarks of Random House, Inc. Bantam Books,
1540 Broadway, New York, New York 10036.

PRINTED IN THE UNITED STATES OF AMERICA

OPM   0 9 8 7 6 5 4 3 2 1

Will Simmons

Okay, so I'm not the most honest guy in the world. I let my friends believe all those lies about Jessica at the beginning of the year, and I even tried to get Ken injured by convincing my friends to let him get sacked. But I came clean in the end—or at least I did something to even the score. But this time I'm not sure honesty is the best policy. Telling the truth about Ken's scholarship—that his father bribed someone to get it for him—wouldn't even the score for anyone. It would just screw things up for Ken, and I feel like I've already done enough of that. So what am I supposed to do?

Conner McDermott

Alanna's drinking again. I know she is. I smelled the alcohol on her breath, I saw the open bottle in her dad's study, and I know she was lying when she said she hadn't had any. But for some reason, I can't just walk away. The problem is I can't stay either.

Evan Plummer

Okay, so it's winter break. Big deal. It's not like I'll be spending the time with my girlfriend since I don't have one. I'll probably just be hanging around with my lazy friends doing nothing, wondering how my life got so pathetic this year. At least Conner's not angry at me anymore, so I have one more lazy friend to sit at home and do nothing with.

Jeremy Aames

My mom, my dad, and my two little sisters are on a plane right now, getting ready to move into a new town in a new state and start a new life there. Tomorrow they'll be moving all their stuff into a new house in a new neighborhood, and they're going to have to do it all without my help because I stayed behind. But I don't feel at all guilty.

Yeah, right.

"Hmmm . . . a *movie* about pool after an entire day of *playing* pool," she said, pretending to consider it as she racked the balls. "I think I'll pass. Six hours is my daily pool limit—in fact, I may have already met my quota for the rest of winter break."

"Yeah, I guess you've got a point." Andy chuckled. He zoomed the last two balls across the table to Tia, then flopped down onto one of the bright orange velour couches his mom had bought at a garage sale to help furnish the rec room. "And actually I've had enough pool too—I was down here shooting around last night too. At least *you* had a date."

Tia scrunched her eyebrows together. "A *date?*" she repeated, staring at Andy, who had sunk into the sofa so comfortably, he might as well have been part of it. "It was *not* a date."

Andy cocked his head and raised his eyebrows. "You went out, didn't you?"

"Yeah, but—"

"With a guy you kissed a while ago?"

Tia rolled her eyes. "Yes," she admitted. "But—"

"Sounds like a date to me," Andy concluded.

Tia folded her arms across her chest. "Are you finished?"

"Depends," Andy said, raising one shoulder. "What kind of lame line are you planning to give me next?"

Tia picked up a neon green pillow from the corner of the couch and hurled it at Andy's head. "I'm not giving you a line," she said, trying to sound firm, but she couldn't help giggling at the way the pillow had skewed Andy's mass of red hair.

"It really wasn't a date," Tia continued, perching cross-legged on the arm of the sofa. "I mean, Trent was there, but Jess and Jeremy were there too, so it was like I was just hanging out with friends. It wasn't like Trent and I were *together* or anything."

"Did you dance?" Andy asked.

"*Hello*—it was the Riot," Tia scoffed. "Of course I danced."

"With Trent?" Andy continued, a mischievous smile playing on his lips.

Tia looked around for another pillow, but Andy had already stuffed both of them behind his back. She glared at him and blew a wispy hair off her forehead. "Okay," she said finally. "*Yes*, I danced with Trent, but . . . sheesh, Andy—*qué pasa?* Why won't you let this go?"

"Because you still like him."

"I do not—" Tia started, but there was no point in continuing. "You know, Andy, sometimes it sucks that you know me so well."

"Believe me, I know," Andy said. "Don't think it didn't bug me that *you* knew I was gay before *I* did.

4

But still, if we didn't know each other so well, we never would have won that *romantic* carriage ride through Central Park."

Tia grinned, remembering how she and Andy had duped the producers of *Test Your Love* into believing that they were boyfriend and girlfriend and how they had beat out the rest of the couples to win the grand-prize trip to New York.

"Yeah, that was pretty cool," she agreed. "Even if it is kind of pathetic that the most romantic moment I've had in months was with you."

"Which is exactly my point," Andy said. He slid over until he was right next to Tia and took her hand, gazing into her eyes with mock sincerity. "I'm gay, Tia, and you can let me win at pool as much as you want, but this relationship just isn't going any further." Tia giggled and tried to jerk her hand away, but Andy held on. "You're going to have to get me out of your head and move on," he finished.

"I'll try," Tia said, pretending to wipe away a tear.

"Seriously, though," Andy said as he pulled away. "You should go for it with Trent. He's cute, he's fun, he's a football player. . . ."

"Yeah, I know," Tia said with a sigh. "Plus he can *dance*, Andy. He actually kept up with me and everything."

"So what's the problem?" Andy asked.

Tia slid down onto the cushion next to Andy and rested her head on his shoulder. "I don't know," she said. "I guess I sort of feel like I already blew it with him once. You know—that whole mess with him and Angel before?"

"Yeah," Andy said, tilting his head to one side. "But if he's still hanging out with you—and dancing with you—he can't be too upset about that."

"I guess," Tia said. It certainly didn't seem like Trent was avoiding her. Then again, he wasn't exactly bending over backward to run into her either.

"So . . . ?" Andy prodded.

"So . . . I don't know. I guess we're just friends, and I'm okay with that."

"Hello—? Tia? You spent a weekend in New York with your gay friend. You went on a couples' game show with your gay friend. You took a romantic carriage ride with your gay friend. At this rate you'll be going to the prom—"

"—with my gay friend," Tia finished. "I know, I know. We talked about this in New York—I don't need any more friends. And I did have a great time with Trent last night, and he is really cute and funny and nice and everything."

"So you'll call him."

Tia took a deep breath. She wasn't sure she was ready to take the next step. "I'll think about it," she

"What? Now?" Jessica asked.

"Not right this minute," Jeremy said, "but yeah, this week. For winter break."

Jessica took a step backward. "You're kidding," she said, studying his face. It was more of a question than a statement.

"Nope. I'm leaving Monday morning, and I could use some company—you know, someone to share the driving, make conversation."

For a moment Jessica just stared, and Jeremy knew she was trying to figure out if he was really serious or not.

"You really mean it, don't you?" Jessica asked.

"Absolutely," Jeremy answered. "I talked to my parents about it right before they left, and they were cool with the idea as long as I could find someone to go with me."

"And you think they had *me* in mind?" Jessica asked, cocking her head.

"Well, no," Jeremy admitted, looking down at his shoes to avoid her gaze. It wasn't like his parents would completely freak out if he made the drive with his girlfriend, but he knew they wouldn't exactly be thrilled. It had been pretty obvious that they expected him to bring along one of his friends. One of his *male* friends. "But I'm sure they'd be okay with it," Jeremy continued.

9

"Especially once they find out that Trent and Stan both can't come."

"Why not?"

"They volunteered to help Coach with the middle-school football camp."

"Oh, that's too bad. The three of you would have had fun," Jessica said.

"Yeah," Jeremy agreed, pulling Jessica close again. "But you and I could have a lot of fun too."

"I know," Jessica said, "but I can't. Even if I could convince my parents that letting me take off for a week with my boyfriend was a good idea, which I actually might be able to do—they really like you, you know—it wouldn't matter. We already have plans. There's this huge Wakefield family reunion going on this week upstate—my dad's entire side of the family is going to be there, and my parents have already booked our rooms."

Jeremy sighed. This wasn't working out the way it was supposed to. Here he was with a great opportunity for a road trip, and no one could go with him. And if he couldn't find someone else to come along, his parents would probably tell him to wait for spring break, when they could fly him out.

"We haven't gotten the whole family together for years," Jessica went on. "I know it sounds kind of boring, but I'm actually really looking forward to it."

"No, it sounds like fun," Jeremy said halfheartedly. Unlike a lot of his friends, he had always been really close to his family, so he understood how a family reunion could be exciting. Too bad he wasn't going to be having one of his own.

"Oh, wait!" Jessica said suddenly, her eyes lighting up.

"What?"

"I know who could go with you."

Jeremy frowned. "Who?"

"Evan!" Jessica blurted. "He'd be perfect!"

"Evan Plummer?" Jeremy asked. Jessica nodded enthusiastically.

Jeremy had met Evan briefly at House of Java, but they'd hardly spoken three words to each other. "I barely know him," Jeremy protested. "What makes you think he'd want to hop in a car and travel a thousand miles with me?"

"I just got off the phone with him," Jessica answered. "Five minutes before you got here. And he was talking about how he wanted to get out of Sweet Valley this week and how he wished he had somewhere to go."

Jeremy squinted as he considered the possibility. "And you think he'd just drive off to Arizona with me?"

"Definitely," Jessica said with a giggle. "Evan's sort of a . . . *free spirit*, I guess you could say."

Hmmm . . . free spirit, Jeremy thought. He wasn't sure if that was a good thing or a bad thing.

"I'm not sure, Jess," he hedged. "I mean, that's a lot of time in the car with someone I don't know very well. What if we don't get along?"

Jessica laughed. "Evan gets along with *everyone.* He's just one of those people that's so mellow and laid-back, you can't help liking him."

Jeremy folded his arms across his chest and shifted his weight from one foot to the other. *It would be too weird,* he thought. He couldn't see himself driving almost a thousand miles and spending a week with someone who was a virtual stranger. Just as he was about to tell Jessica no, Elizabeth walked out of the kitchen.

"Hi, Jeremy," she called on her way through the hallway and toward the stairs.

"Liz!" Jessica shouted after her. Elizabeth turned and walked back over to them. "Tell Jeremy what a nice guy Evan Plummer is," Jessica said.

"Nicest guy I've ever met—next to you, of course, Jeremy," Elizabeth said, smiling.

Jeremy snorted. "Thanks," he returned sarcastically.

"And how do you think he'd be on a road trip with Jeremy—to Arizona?"

Elizabeth pressed her lips together. "Are you driving out to Arizona?" she asked Jeremy.

"Yeah, to help my family get settled."

"But only if he can find someone to go with him," Jessica added.

"Oh, I get it," Elizabeth said. She paused, then nodded slowly. "Well, then Evan would be perfect. He's very *low maintenance*. Really mellow, fun, easy to get along with . . ."

"What did I tell you?" Jessica said smugly, one hand on her hip.

Jeremy looked from Jessica to Elizabeth and back again. "Why do I feel like I've just been ambushed?"

"Jessica has that effect on people," Elizabeth said, dodging a retaliatory shoulder punch from her sister. "Can I go now?" she asked.

"Please," Jessica answered, waving one hand toward the stairs. "So," she began, turning back to Jeremy. "What are you going to do?"

"I don't know," Jeremy said with a sigh.

"You need someone to go with you, right?"

"Yeah."

"And even Liz—who is ten times more straight arrow than you could ever be—thinks Evan would be cool to travel with."

"Yeah," Jeremy agreed.

"So you'll call him?" Jessica asked hopefully.

Jeremy tried to think of someone else he could ask—anyone—but he couldn't. Most of the guys

13

from the team were either helping out with the camp or going away with their own families. It looked like Evan might be his last chance.

"Yeah," he said finally. "I'll call him."

"Good," Jessica said, beaming. "I'm sure you'll have fun—and I think it's really cool that you'll be getting to know one of my friends so well."

Jeremy nodded and tried to relax. After all, if Evan was really as easy to get along with as Jessica and Elizabeth said, he had absolutely nothing to worry about.

"To Sweet Valley's championship win and the quarterback who made it happen." Mr. Matthews raised his wineglass and touched it to Ken's—which contained sparkling cider, then Maria's—cranberry juice and ginger ale. When Ken glanced at Maria and clinked her glass, he felt like his smile must be on the verge of taking over his entire face.

She looked even more amazing tonight than usual—her bold, dark eyes gleaming in the candlelit dining room of the restaurant. She was wearing a dress he'd never seen her in before—this long, dark blue slinky thing that showed off her perfect body.

"Congratulations," Maria said, smiling sweetly at him. "On the game and the scholarship."

"Thanks," Ken said, aware that the goofy grin was

still plastered across his face. But there was nothing he could do about it. Between winning the game last night and having Hank Krubowski confirm that he was getting a full football scholarship to U. Michigan, he was soaring.

"And congratulations to you too, Maria," Mr. Matthews added.

Maria blinked rapidly. "For what?" she asked, obviously startled. Ken sucked in his breath, suddenly anxious. It would be just like his father to say something lame and ruin the festive mood that had been with them all night.

"For winning the Senate scholarship," Mr. Matthews said. "I realize it was a little while ago, but I don't think I ever got the chance to congratulate you properly. So—this dinner is for you too."

"Oh," Maria said. She shot a glance at Ken and then turned back to his father. "Well, thank you." She smiled quickly at Mr. Matthews, then began fidgeting with her napkin in her lap.

It was obvious she hardly knew what to say, and Ken was equally dumbfounded. His father hadn't always gone out of his way to be nice to Maria—probably because he thought she had something to do with Ken's giving up football for a brief period at the beginning of the school year, simply because they had started dating around the same time that Ken left the team. Ken had told his father numerous times that Maria had nothing to do with his decision, but Mr. Matthews had never quite seemed to believe him.

But tonight it was different. It was as if everything had finally fallen into place and none of that old stuff mattered at all anymore. In fact, everything seemed to be going perfectly.

"The two of you are really racking up the scholarships," Mr. Matthews observed, causing both Ken and Maria to chuckle. "I'm very proud of both of you."

Okay, Dad, Ken thought. *Let's not take it too far.* He thought Maria might be getting a little uncomfortable with all the praise. She didn't seem to be looking Mr. Matthews in the eye anymore. But almost as if he had heard his son's thoughts, Mr. Matthews changed tacks.

"Any word from Yale yet, Maria?" he asked.

"No, not yet," Maria said, scrunching up her nose. "But it shouldn't be too much longer."

"Well, don't sweat it," Mr. Matthews said. "Waiting is the hardest part, but I'm sure you'll get in. What are you planning to major in?"

"Prelaw, with a concentration in black history," Maria answered. "I'm hoping to be a civil-rights litigator eventually," she added, her voice taking on a

16

more natural tone now. Ken was amazed. His father had managed to put Maria at ease, and now they were talking at length about her future plans—and Mr. Matthews was showing sincere interest.

Again the wide smile spread across Ken's face, and he realized he felt happier than he had in a long time. Somehow everything had worked out. He was playing the sport he loved, and he would be for four more years now at a top school—which was totally paid for by his scholarship. His father—whom he'd felt so distant from just a few weeks ago—was actually sitting here treating both Ken and Maria with respect, and he was actually *proud* of Ken. And to top it all off, Ken had Maria back in his life. That was really the best part too—more important than anything else.

Ken took a sip from his water glass and considered how much things had changed for him in such a short time. Not long ago, it seemed that everything in his life was going wrong. But *now*—well, now it all seemed almost too good to be true.

"I don't believe this," Conner said, throwing up his hands in disgust. "Do you realize none of those guys can even play an instrument?"

"They don't need to, man," Evan said, leaning back against the plush brown cushions of his living-room

17

sofa and clasping his hands behind his head. "No one cares whether they can play or not—only how cute they are and how well they can dance."

Conner rolled his eyes. "I just wish they'd play some music by someone who could pick a guitar out of a lineup."

"Conner—this is MTV. It's not about talent. It's about image." Evan waved a hand toward the screen. "I mean, these guys can sing okay, but they weren't *discovered* for their voices. You could find fifty guys at SVH who could sing just as well with a little training." Conner shrugged one shoulder and scowled at the TV while Evan snagged a few chips from the bag on the coffee table and gulped them down.

"Nope, these guys aren't about talent," Evan continued.

"You're telling me," Conner grumbled.

"They're about image. Appearance over substance. It's what everybody wants. No one cares who you are or what you're really all about—only which jeans you're wearing and what kind of car you drive. It's a major American flaw, you know—we prefer the packaging over what's actually inside. The brand name instead of the generic alternative, even though it has all the same ingredients."

"Okay, here we go," Conner murmured as the title of the song, the band's name, and all the other information came up on the screen, signaling that the video was almost over. Evan watched as his friend stared at the TV, clenching and unclenching his jaw, virtually willing a decent song to begin.

"Oh, come on," Conner practically shouted as a new video started. This time there was a huge logo flashing on the screen: All Boy Bands, All Weekend. "This has to be a joke," he said, sinking into Mr. Plummer's well-worn La-Z-Boy and folding his arms across his chest.

Evan couldn't help chuckling as he reached for the remote and clicked off the TV. "It's fate, man," he replied, shaking his head. Conner scowled at him. "I'm serious," Evan continued. "Think about it—what's the last thing you wanted to see just now?"

"That," Conner sneered, nodding toward the now blank television screen.

"Exactly. If a band you really liked had come on, we'd still be sitting here watching TV."

"So?"

"*So*," Evan said, leaning forward and resting his elbows on his knees, "we're not. Instead we're going to come up with some way to get out of here for the rest of winter break."

Conner eyed him suspiciously. "Out of *where?*"

"Out of Sweet Valley, my friend," Evan said. "I don't

know about you, but I need to put some distance between myself and this town."

"I know what you mean," Conner mumbled. His intense green eyes seemed to be focused on something a thousand miles away, and Evan knew exactly what it was—Alanna Feldman. Evan sighed. It didn't seem like either of them had been having the best luck with relationships lately. Evan had seriously bombed three times in a row, and Conner's track record wasn't much better.

"Maybe we could—" Evan started, but he was interrupted by the phone ringing. He leaned across the sofa and grabbed the portable. "Hello?" he answered.

"Hi, Evan?"

"Yep," Evan replied. He frowned, wondering who it was—the voice wasn't familiar at all.

"This is Jeremy. Jeremy *Aames*. Jessica's boyfriend."

"Oh—hey, man. How's it going?"

Conner nodded toward the phone, silently asking who it was, but Evan ignored him. Why would Jeremy be calling him? Was something wrong with Jessica?

"Um, I know this is going to sound kind of strange—since we've never really hung out or anything, but . . ."

The silence was palpable, and Evan could practically

feel Jeremy's discomfort through the phone. "That's okay—I like strange," he joked. He didn't know Jeremy well at all, but he'd heard enough from Jessica—and Jade, for that matter—to know he was all right. "So what's up?"

"Well, I don't know how much Jessica's told you about me, but the rest of my family just moved out to Arizona."

"Yeah, Jessica mentioned that—but you're finishing out the year here, right?"

"Right, except I was hoping to drive out and help them get settled this week, which is why I'm calling."

Evan was still puzzled, and obviously Conner was too. He was looking over at Evan with his face in full scowl mode.

"I need someone to make the drive with me," Jeremy continued, "and when I mentioned it to Jessica, she said she thought you might be up for a road trip." At the sound of the words *road trip*, Evan's entire face lit up, causing Conner's scowl to deepen even further.

"Yeah, well, Jessica was right," he said eagerly. He got up and started pacing across the room. "I'm definitely up for it—what's the plan? I mean, when do you want to leave?"

"Uh—don't you need to ask your parents or something?" Jeremy asked, his voice cautious.

"Oh, yeah," Evan said, waving a hand dismissively

21

even though Jeremy couldn't see him. "But that's no big deal—they'll be cool with it."

"Oh. Okay. Well, then, I guess we leave Monday morning. I was thinking around eight-thirty?"

"Sounds good," Evan said, feeling the grin on his face spread through his entire body. A road trip. How cool! It was exactly what he needed to clear his head. He glanced over at Conner, who had reclined the La-Z-Boy and closed his eyes. He had apparently tired of trying to guess who Evan was talking to.

"Hey," Evan said, suddenly struck by an idea. "How about one more person? You know—to split the driving up a little more, help pay for gas?" Conner's eyes popped open, and he looked over at Evan.

"Um, I don't know. I mean, I guess that would be okay," Jeremy hedged.

"Great," Evan said. "I'll have Conner meet us here on Monday morning at—what did you say? Eight-thirty?" Conner stood up and moved closer to Evan. He was scrutinizing his friend now, his eyes reduced to narrow slits, but his indignant expression only made Evan's grin widen. He knew Conner would be psyched once he understood, but Evan wasn't in any hurry to fill him in. It was kind of fun to watch his friend squirm with discomfort for a while.

"Okay," Jeremy agreed, his voice slow and tentative. "Um, did you say, *Conner?*"

"Yeah—do you know him?"

"Only through Jessica," Jeremy returned, and all at once Evan understood why he sounded so uncomfortable.

"Oh," he said with a chuckle. "Well, don't believe everything Jessica says about him. He's not *that* bad." Conner was positively sneering now—he clearly didn't enjoy being talked about as if he wasn't in the room. "In fact," Evan continued, "he's kind of lovable once you get to know him." Conner rolled his eyes and flopped back into the chair, and Evan could tell from the silence on the phone that his last comment hadn't done much to make Jeremy feel better either.

"All right," Jeremy said. "So, I'll pick you up Monday morning at—"

"Seventy-seven Wilmot Drive," Evan finished for him. "Do you know where that is?"

"Yeah, I think so. Isn't Wilmot off Graham Street—right after the deli?"

"That's the one. We'll be waiting outside—oh, and are we going for the week? I'll need to tell my mom and dad when we're coming back."

"Oh, right. I was planning to come back Friday— you know, take the weekend to recover."

"Sounds good," Evan said. "So I'll talk to my parents and call you back if I have any questions, okay?"

23

"Okay. Thanks, man," Jeremy said, his voice still sounding uncertain.

That's okay, Evan thought. Jeremy was bound to loosen up once they hit the road and he had a chance to see that Conner wasn't the jerk Jessica had made him out to be. At least, not completely.

"What was that about?" Conner snapped once Evan had hung up the phone.

"We're going on a road trip," Evan said, patting his friend's shoulder.

"We're *what?*" Conner asked.

"Going on a road trip," Evan repeated. He ducked into the hallway and pulled a big duffel bag out of the storage closet. "With Jeremy Aames—Jessica's boyfriend," he said as he reentered the living room. Conner gave him a blank look. "You know—tall guy, short black hair—he goes to Big Mesa, works at House of Java? Football player—really clean cut?"

Conner nodded. "But how do you know him?"

"I don't," Evan said with a shrug, "at least, not really. But he's driving out to see his family in Arizona, and we're going with him."

"Oh, we are, are we?" Conner sneered. "How did that come about?"

"Simple. He invited me, I invited you." Conner rolled his eyes. "Come on, McD.," Evan persuaded. "You know you need to get away. And it's our senior

24

year. Next semester we're going to have to start making all those really big future decisions about what we're going to do with our lives—don't you want to get out and live a little first?" Conner shrugged, and Evan knew he was right on the edge. "Hey—there's nothing like a little road trip to clear your head—free your mind so you can come back and attack things from a fresh perspective. How could you possibly pass on this?"

Conner exhaled heavily. "Look, even if I said yes, there's no way my mother would let me go. Not after . . . you know, everything that's been going on."

Evan nodded, remembering what it had been like to watch his friend lose control. But Conner had been to rehab, and he was taking care of himself now. Evan couldn't believe how much better Conner already seemed from just a couple of months ago.

"*I'll* talk to your mother," Evan offered. "I'll convince her this would be good for you. She *loves* me—you know that."

"Yeah, she thinks you're really mature and responsible," Conner said, squinting. "Though I don't know why."

"Because I am," Evan said matter-of-factly.

"Right," Conner scoffed. But Evan could tell he was getting his point across.

"So you're in?" Evan asked.

"Yeah, I'm in. If you can convince my mom."

"No problem," Evan said, grabbing a pair of sneakers off the floor and stuffing them in his duffel. Then he threw back his head and laughed. "This is going to be great!" he said. "It's exactly what we need—a chance to let loose and go wild."

Evan grinned at his friend, and Conner actually cracked a small smile. "Just don't use that argument with my mother, okay?" Conner said.

"No worries," Evan reassured him. "No worries."

Jeremy Aames

Itinerary for Arizona Trip

Monday

8:30 A.M.	0 miles	Leave Evan's; Jeremy driving
9:45 A.M.	45 miles	Quick coffee break/rest stop before hitting highway
1:00 P.M.	223 miles	Lunch
1:30 P.M.		Back on road; Evan driving
3:15 P.M.	330 miles	Quick rest break
3:30 P.M.		On highway
4:30 P.M.	375 miles	Rest/snack break
4:45 P.M.		Back on road; Conner driving
7:00 P.M.	486 miles	Cross state line; get dinner; head for parents.

Okay, so it's a little tight, but with three drivers we should be able to do it. I just hope Jessica was right about Evan being really easy to travel with. And I hope she was totally wrong when she told me that Conner McDermott was the biggest jerk she'd ever met in her life.

CHAPTER

DÉJÀ VU

2

"I'll have Rocky Road, and . . ." Will turned to face Melissa.

"White chocolate frozen yogurt," she said, fixing the cute girl behind the counter with one of her stony glares. Then she wrapped herself around Will's right arm and rested her head on his shoulder. Will sighed. Melissa was always hyperaffectionate when there was an attractive girl within a five-mile radius. It would have bothered him coming from anyone else, but he was pretty used to Melissa's insecurities by now.

After Will paid, they walked outside to the round tables with their bright blue-and-white umbrellas and took a seat.

"Mmmm," Will said, swallowing a mouthful of ice cream. "This is good." He paused, gazing around the area. "It's really nice out today," he said. "Yesterday was kind of cool, but today is perfect. And my mom said this morning that the whole

28

week's supposed to be like this." He took another bite of his ice cream, then glanced over at Melissa. She was giving him one of her trademark penetrating stares.

"Okay. Why are you going on and on about the weather?" she asked, her voice taking on a slight edge.

Will hesitated. He knew exactly what Melissa wanted to talk about, but there was no way he was going to bring it up. "I don't know," he said with a shrug. "Just because it's a nice day, I guess."

Melissa rolled her eyes. "Are you just going to keep avoiding the subject?"

"What subject?" Will asked, stalling for time. He needed to find some way to successfully lie to Melissa about what he'd seen take place between Ken Matthews's father and Hank Krubowski on Friday night. Melissa had been trying to get the information out of him all weekend, but so far Will had managed to dodge her questions—or actually, Melissa had *allowed* him to dodge her questions. Obviously she'd reached her limit with that.

"All right," Melissa said after a moment of silence. "I want the truth about Ken's scholarship."

It was classic Melissa—straight to the point. And her eyes were equally direct, which was going to make it nearly impossible to lie to her. Still, Will knew he had to give it a shot. He hadn't decided how he wanted to handle things with Mr. Matthews yet, and until he figured that out, he really didn't want to tell anyone else what he had heard.

"What makes you think *I'd* know anything about it?" he asked, returning Melissa's unwavering gaze and trying to hold it. Liars always looked away.

Melissa cocked her head. "I'm not stupid, Will. You told me last week that you were pretty sure something was going on between Ken's dad and Hank Krubowski. Then Ken completely blows the championship game, looking like an idiot on the field, and Krubowski still gives him the scholarship to Michigan? Come on." Her blue eyes narrowed a degree further. Will couldn't help thinking what a great police interrogator Melissa would make. And as much as he hated being the subject of her scrutiny, he knew deep down that her sharp mind was one of the things he admired most about his girlfriend.

"You've been acting weird ever since we left the game Friday night," Melissa continued. "So tell me the truth—was Ken's scholarship rigged or what?"

Will blinked and stared back at the ice cream shop. An elderly couple was emerging from the front door hand in hand. He turned back to Melissa.

"Come on, Liss," he began, hoping he could still

put this off. "It's a perfect Sunday afternoon, and we've got a whole two weeks off—"

"*You* don't have the time off," Melissa reminded him. "You've got your internship."

"Yeah, I guess," Will said. Mr. Matthews had offered to give him more hours at the paper during winter break, and Will had jumped at the chance. But now he was beginning to regret it. How was he even supposed to look Mr. Matthews in the eye after what he'd heard outside the snack booth Friday night?

"I'll have my nights free," Will offered, but Melissa just shrugged. Will knew he had to plunge forward if he was going to convince her. "All I'm saying is, we've got a great break ahead of us—why waste time talking about Ken Matthews and his stupid scholarship?"

Melissa leaned back and crossed her arms. "What you're *really* saying is that you don't trust me enough to tell me the truth."

Will resisted the urge to roll his eyes and groan. "No—that's not it, Liss. I just mean . . . what's it matter how Ken got the scholarship anyway? He got it, end of story."

The corner of Melissa's mouth curved upward slightly, and Will knew he'd made a serious mistake. "So it *was* fixed," she said. "But how? Did Mr.

Matthews actually *pay* Krubowski to give Ken the scholarship?"

Will shook his head. There was no point in even trying to deny it anymore—Melissa wasn't going to let it go until she knew the whole story.

"No, he didn't pay him," Will mumbled, staring down at the ground. Somehow it was easier to tell her if he didn't make eye contact.

"What, then?" Melissa asked.

Will swallowed hard. "I guess Ken's dad has some influence at another college athletic department, so he promised Krubowski he could get him a coaching job next fall if Hank came through with the scholarship for Ken."

Melissa shook her head. "Unbelievable. I mean, not that the whole thing was fixed—I knew Ken didn't deserve that scholarship. But his father actually *bribed* the scout? That's pathetic. And Ken likes to act like he's such a Boy Scout too. Whatever."

"I don't know," Will said, shifting in his seat. "I don't really want to talk about it. The whole thing just makes me feel queasy."

"I can see why," Melissa jumped in. "That was *your* scholarship. You would have—"

"It's not that," Will interrupted. Didn't Melissa get it? He had to go to the *Tribune* tomorrow and work side by side with Ken's dad, which meant he either had to confront Mr. Matthews about the bribe or admit to himself that he could be bought off too. After all, Mr. Matthews was the one who had gotten him the internship. If Will came clean with what he knew about the scholarship, he might as well kiss his spot at the *Tribune* good-bye.

"Well, what is it, then?" Melissa asked.

Will shook his head. "Really—let's just talk about something else."

"Okay," Melissa said, her face softening.

"And Liss?"

"Yeah?"

"Promise you won't tell anyone about this?"

Melissa tilted her head and smiled. "Don't worry," she said soothingly. But her answer just made him worry more. After all, she'd dodged his question expertly.

Just as Tia was about to take her seat at the dinner table with the rest of her family on Sunday night, the doorbell rang, blaring through their one-story home.

"I'll get it," she said, jumping back up and hurrying out of the room. Her mother didn't bother to stop her. Probably because everyone at the table suspected it was one of her friends. Tia's parents were both excellent cooks, and her friends all knew it.

They had a habit of showing up precisely at dinnertime, knowing there was always enough to go around at the Ramirez house.

As Tia bounded toward the door, she tried to guess who it would be. She'd been hanging out with Andy all weekend, so it probably wasn't him. *But Conner hasn't been by in a while,* she thought.

She swung open the door, already opening her mouth to tease Conner for showing up at dinnertime. But when she saw who was there, her mouth just hung open, and she couldn't form a single word for at least a couple of seconds.

"Angel," she finally got out, feeling a million emotions swirl through her as the word pushed itself out of her throat. "What—what are you doing here?"

Angel smiled. "College students get winter break too," he said. "I'm in town for a little while."

"Oh, *duh*," Tia said. Why hadn't it occurred to her that he'd be coming home? "Of course you do. So . . . what's up?" Tia stared into his brown eyes, shocked by how nervous she was to see him. Although it wasn't nervous as much as it was excited. Which was totally weird since they'd broken up months ago and she was convinced she was totally over him. Or at least she had been convinced— right up until she'd opened the door and found him standing on her front porch.

34

"Not much. I just thought I'd see what you were up to, how things were going," he replied.

Tia nodded dumbly.

"So?" he said, arching his eyebrows.

Tia gave him a blank look. "So . . . *what?*"

"*So,* what have you been up to?" Angel asked, and there was that charming smile again.

"Oh, yeah." Tia laughed nervously. His sudden appearance in her life again had totally thrown her off—as had her thumping heart and racing pulse. Why was she getting so wacked out over an old boyfriend who was just a friend now? *Maybe because you still think of him as more than a friend,* she told herself.

"Um, not much, really," she managed finally. "I mean, I've e-mailed you about most of the stuff that's happened since you left—except the whole Senate scholarship thing, but that's a long story—"

"So why don't we get together and you can fill me in?" Angel suggested.

Tia felt a shiver run through her body and realized she had visibly trembled. "It must be cooling off," she muttered, even though she knew it wasn't true.

"So what do you think? Dinner? A movie?" he asked.

"Um, sure," Tia blurted automatically. As usual her mouth was ten steps ahead of her brain. *What are you thinking?* she yelled at herself. It was obvious

35

she was still attracted to Angel, no matter how much she had tried to deny it, but was going out with him really the smartest thing to do?

"So," Angel said, stuffing his hands in his front pockets. "Are you, uh, seeing anybody?"

"No," Tia said. Suddenly it hit her—Angel had a girlfriend. He really was just asking to hang out with her, nothing more. Wasn't she supposed to be relieved at that? Somehow relief wasn't quite among the emotions she was experiencing.

"Me neither," he said.

Tia took in a quick burst of air. "But what about that girl you told me about? You said you guys were—"

Angel shrugged. "We broke up a few weeks ago. It just wasn't going anywhere."

"Oh," Tia said. Hmmm . . . there was that relief now. "That's too bad," she lied. Then almost immediately she started giggling—she couldn't help it. To her surprise, Angel began laughing too.

"You never were very good at hiding your feelings," he said, still chuckling.

"I know." Tia sighed, wiping away the tears that had formed at the corners of her eyes.

"So—how about tomorrow night? I'm doing some work for my dad at his garage, but I should be done by five. I could pick you up around six."

"That sounds good," Tia said with a grin. Finally her nerves were beginning to calm down.

"Tia! Dinner!"

Tia shook her head at the sound of her mother's voice screaming for her. Her family was probably dying to start eating, but they'd be waiting for her to join them, like always.

"Gotta go," she told Angel. "But I'll see you tomorrow?"

"Yeah, tomorrow," he said. He flashed her one last smile, then turned to go. Tia headed back toward the dining room, glancing up at the clock on the living-room wall as she passed it. Only twenty-three hours, fifty-eight minutes, and fifteen seconds between her and a date with Angel.

"Michigan is going to be so cool," Ken said, removing a piece of pizza from the cardboard box on Maria's coffee table. "It's right in the middle of the city, so it's close to everything, but it's still got a really green campus." He took a huge bite off the end of his slice and grinned at Maria.

"Yeah, I've seen pictures of their campus," Maria agreed. "One of my sister's friends went there. It *is* really pretty—and Ann Arbor seems like a fun city."

"Mmm-hmm," Ken said, gulping down another bite of pizza. "I haven't been there, but I've heard it's got everything. In the brochure it says there are like twelve museums nearby and a bunch of theaters—not to mention all the football I'm going to be able to see. Detroit's practically next door, and Browns and Packers games would only be day trips."

"Wow, it's like the heartland of football out there," Maria said, blinking rapidly.

"Yeah—isn't it great! I'm *so* psyched," Ken said, diving into another piece of pizza.

Maria giggled. "Really?" she teased. "I never would have guessed." She took a sip of her iced tea, replacing the glass on one of the crystal coasters her mother had set strategically around the room.

"I'm sorry," Ken said, realizing he'd been babbling about the University of Michigan ever since they had gone to pick up the pizza—forty-five minutes ago. He set down his pizza slice and edged closer to Maria on the sofa. "You must be getting sick of hearing about U. Mich."

"Not at all," Maria said. "I'm glad you got that scholarship, and I'm glad you're so excited about it." Ken gave her a little squeeze—she was always so supportive. "In fact," Maria continued, "I'd probably be babbling on and on about Yale right now if I'd heard anything from them."

Right. Yale. As in, one of the colleges Maria wanted to go to—one of the colleges she liked that all happened to be pretty far away from Michigan. Suddenly

Ken realized that this could easily turn into one of those conversations about how hard it was going to be to go their separate ways at the end of the summer.

"Don't even go there," Maria said, narrowing her dark eyes at him.

Ken frowned. "What?" he said.

"I said, don't even go there," Maria repeated. "I can see it all over your face, but you don't need to worry. I'm not going to get all weepy and sentimental about going away to college. At least, not yet."

Ken's eyebrows shot up. She really had read his mind.

"Ken, you know how I feel about you," she began. "I'm really glad we got back together, and yeah, it might be hard to say good-bye when the time comes. But college is still like eight months away—that's three-quarters of a year. We've got tons of time, and right now I just want to be happy for you." Maria took a bite of her pizza, then washed it down with some iced tea. "*Now*, if you still want to start the movie, you can go right ahead. But if you'd rather rave about U. Michigan and how excited you are for a little while longer, that's fine too. After all, when I get my acceptance letter from Yale, you're going to have to listen to me babble for a long time."

Ken could only stare, dumbfounded, for a couple of seconds. Then he leaned over, wrapped one arm around Maria to pull her closer, and kissed her.

"Mmmm," Maria said, her eyes still closed. "What was that for?"

"For being the best girlfriend in the world," Ken answered, and he leaned in and kissed her again.

To: tee@swiftnet.com
From: trent#1@cal.rr.com
Subject: What's up?

Hi, Tia—

What's up? Not much on my end, except Jeremy's leaving for Arizona tomorrow. He asked me and Stan to drive out with him, but we're both doing this football-clinic thing with Coach Anderson, so I'm stuck hanging around here this week. How about you? Are you doing anything exciting? If you get bored, you can always come down to the middle school—Stan and I could teach you blocking techniques or something.

See ya,
Trent

To: trent#1@cal.rr.com
From: tee@swiftnet.com
Subject: re: what's up?

hey trent—

did you say <u>blocking techniques?</u>
trust me, with three little brothers
i've already got plenty of those—in
fact, I could probably teach you and
stan a thing or two!

as for break, no, I don't have
anything big planned either, unless
you consider working for free in my
parents' deli exciting. oh, and I did
play eight hours of pool in andy's
basement yesterday. hmmm . . . that
football clinic's beginning to sound
more and more exciting . . . maybe I
will stop by! :-)

talk to you later!

adios,
tia

To: marsden1@swiftnet.com
From: tee@swiftnet.com
Subject: angel!

hey pool shark!
   you'll never guess who stopped by
tonight just as we were about to have
dinner, except I guess you can tell
from the subject of this message. can
you believe it? it was weird to see him
again at first—like total déjà vu—but
it turns out he's on break too, and he
actually asked me if I wanted to go out
tomorrow night for dinner and a movie.
it looks like there's still something
between us after all. and you wanted me
to call trent . . . oh, well, i'll
forgive you. this time. :-)
   just kidding—I know you were only
looking out for me, but now that
angel's home, it looks like you won't
need to anymore. now we just have to
find a guy for you. hey—what do you
think the chances are that conner's
gay? it's not like he's ever been
able to keep a girlfriend for more
than two weeks. . . .

                         love,
                         t

CHAPTER
On the Road
3

"Everything's going to be fine," Jeremy told himself as he turned left on Wilmot Avenue early Monday morning. But even as he said it, he noticed his palms were beginning to feel a little sweaty on the steering wheel.

All night long he'd had nightmares about making the drive with Evan and Conner. In the first one they'd been driving for four hours without ever managing to leave Sweet Valley. In another, when Jeremy showed up at Evan's to pick them up, they weren't around. He checked the house and waited outside for a while, but there was no sign of them. Then, when he started to pull away, both of them came running from out of nowhere, racing toward the car with petrified looks on their faces. They jumped in without even waiting for Jeremy to come to a complete stop, and Evan yelled, "Drive!" So for the rest of the dream—which seemed to go on forever—Jeremy had driven like a madman along twisting mountain roads without ever knowing why.

But those were just dreams, Jeremy told himself, gripping the steering wheel a little harder as he scanned each house and mailbox for street numbers. *Fifty-three, fifty-five, fifty-seven,* he noted, but there was no need to count any further. In the distance he could see Evan and Conner waiting on the side of the road, their duffel bags piled beside them.

"I guess that's a good sign," Jeremy told himself, realizing he'd half expected them to still be asleep. When he got closer, he could see that Evan was playing hacky sack with a little blue-and-white ball. Conner stood with one hand jammed into the front pocket of his faded jeans and the other curled around a plastic mug of coffee.

Jeremy pulled up next to the curb just as Evan kicked the hacky sack extra high and then pulled a leather pouch out of the front pocket of his tan shorts, catching the ball inside it.

"Nice move," Jeremy said as he stepped out of the car. Evan smiled and nodded, but before he could reply, Conner stepped forward.

"Nice car," he said, running his hand along the hood of Jeremy's Mercedes.

"It used to be," Jeremy said. His dad had maintained the car meticulously up until a few years ago, when his workload had increased dramatically, leaving him with little time for his favorite hobby. The Mercedes sat in the Aameses' garage—untouched—for a solid year, at which point Mr. Aames had decided to let Jeremy start driving it so it would at least get some use.

"What d'ya mean, '*used to be*'?" Conner asked, walking around to the driver's side.

"Just that it's my dad's old—"

"Sixty-five SEL," Conner murmured, opening the driver's-side door and getting in.

"—car," Jeremy finished. He didn't want to be a jerk, but shouldn't Conner have at least asked before he jumped into the car like that? Jeremy looked at Evan, who just shook his head.

"Don't mind Conner. He completely lacks social grace," Evan explained. "Conner! Hey, don't you think you should say hello first?"

"Huh?" Conner said, glancing over at them. "Oh, yeah. Right." He waved toward Jeremy and nodded slightly. "How's it going?"

Jeremy forced a smile and tried to laugh along with Evan, but his first impression of Conner was that Jessica *had* been right. The guy was a jerk.

"So anyway," Jeremy said, clearing his throat. "We'd better get going. You guys want to throw your stuff in the back?"

"Yeah, sure," Evan said. As he started to lift the

duffels from the ground, Conner hopped out from behind the steering wheel and came around to help. Meanwhile Jeremy reached into the front passenger seat and pulled out two pieces of paper.

"I put this itinerary together last night," he said, handing one sheet to Conner and the other to Evan, then glancing at his watch. "It's eight thirty-five now, so we've already lost five minutes, but we can probably make that up by cutting the first rest break a little short. In fact, I should probably make a note of that now," Jeremy said, reaching back into the car to get his copy of the itinerary. He was trying to find a pen when he heard the laughter.

Slowly he stepped back from the car and turned to face Conner and Evan. They were pointing at various sections of their itineraries and practically howling.

"What? What is it?" Jeremy demanded, narrowing his eyes.

"Nothing," Evan said, struggling to get his breath. He was still chuckling, but it was obvious he was trying really hard to get himself under control. "Really, don't worry about it. We were just noticing how . . . precise you've been with the times." Conner made a strange coughing noise that seemed to be an attempt to cover up more laughter.

Jeremy took a deep breath. *Great. This is just great.* He could hardly wait to thank Jessica for hooking him up with these two clowns for the week.

"Oh, jeez." Evan shook his head. "I'm sorry, man. You're going to have to just ignore us this morning—we were up way too late last night." Jeremy shoved his hands in his pockets and nodded. "No, really," Evan insisted. He walked over and slapped Jeremy on the back. "There's nothing wrong with your schedule. In fact, it's really good—we might even hit a couple of those times."

Conner started to chuckle again, but Evan cast him a quick glance, and he stopped.

"Whatever," Jeremy said. "I'm driving first. Let's get going." Evan and Conner were silent as Jeremy walked over to the driver's side. And at least when Conner reached for the front passenger-side door, Evan nudged him aside. If Jeremy had to have one of them in the shotgun seat, he would have chosen Evan.

Jeremy sighed as he pulled away from the curb. *At least everything didn't start out bad,* he thought. After all, he hadn't had to wake them up.

Will tugged at the crimson tie around his neck, using the steel interior wall of the elevator as a mirror. By the time the doors slid open on the fifth floor of the *Tribune* building, he'd managed to adjust the knot so that the tie lay flat against his crisp white button-down shirt.

Mr. Matthews had told him business casual was fine, but Will had thrown on a tie anyway. It was his first full day as an intern in the sports department, and he wanted to make a good impression on all the journalists he hadn't met yet. It certainly wouldn't hurt to make a few new contacts that might be able to help him with future jobs—especially since this was probably going to be his last day working with Mr. Matthews.

Will exited the elevator as quickly as his bad knee would allow him and headed toward Mr. Matthews's office, his stomach churning with each step. He'd lain awake forever the night before, trying to decide what to do. For a while he'd been convinced that doing nothing was the best idea of all. Then Ken would go to Michigan, Mr. Matthews would be happy, and Will's career in sports journalism would be off to a great start. But in the end he'd come to the conclusion that he had to tell Mr. Matthews what he knew. It was the only way his conscience would ever be clear—not to mention the only way he could be certain that he wasn't being paid off.

As he limped through the hall, Will noticed that things seemed exceptionally busy today. All around him he could hear the clacking of computer keyboards interspersed with ringing phones and bits and pieces of conversations.

He passed two guys in a cubicle who were arguing about which teams would make the play-offs, while in the break room off to the right a woman was demanding to know who ate the last jelly doughnut. Everyone seemed to be hustling around, but the mood was upbeat, and the people all seemed to be having a good time. Will found it energizing—kind of like the talk in a locker room just before a big game. Maybe he really would be a sportswriter someday.

When he finally got to Mr. Matthews's office, he was surprised to see that there were already five or six other people inside—not exactly the perfect setup for bringing up the scholarship issue. Will glanced at his watch. Quarter to nine. Mr. Matthews had told him nine o'clock would be fine, but he hadn't mentioned anything about a meeting.

"Will," Mr. Matthews bellowed, beckoning him into the office. "Just the man we've been waiting for."

Will's shoulders tensed slightly as he entered. "Uh—am I late?"

Mr. Matthews glanced at the clock. "Nope. In fact, you're twelve minutes early—but that's good. I've got an assignment for you." He motioned for Will to come over by his desk while he finished up with the others. Will shuffled his feet along the industrial-grade gray carpet, aware that his blood pressure was rising with every step he took toward

Mr. Matthews. He was dreading what he had to do with every ounce of his body—but his heart and stomach seemed to be taking it the hardest.

"All right—this is what I have," Mr. Matthews said, reading from a notepad in front of him. "Ben will cover the amateur golf tourney out at Riverdale this afternoon, George has UCLA at Stanford, Jenn is covering women's tennis, and—what do you have, Jerry?" he asked, furrowing his brow.

"Big Mesa football clinic."

"That's right," Mr. Matthews said, scribbling something down. "Okay, then—see you all back here around five." The four journalists he had spoken to muttered good-byes as they filtered out the door, leaving only Mr. Matthews, Will, and a woman Will had never met before in the office—which meant Will was going to have to postpone his talk with Mr. Matthews even longer. That is, if his heart didn't give out first.

"Will, this is Meg," Mr. Matthews said, gesturing to the woman. She was about Will's height, with curly dark hair cropped at the shoulder and dark brown eyes. She seemed to be in her midthirties. "Meg—Will."

"Glad to meet you," Meg said, extending her hand. Will reached out, expecting a limp handshake, but Meg's grasp was firm.

"The two of you will be working together today,"
Mr. Matthews said. "The Forty Niners are holding a
closed practice session this afternoon to prep for
their big game next Sunday, but they've agreed to let
Meg and a few other reporters in to do some interviews. I thought you could go with her."

Will's brain was on overdrive as he tried to
process everything he'd just heard. "Wait—Forty
Niners?" he said. "As in *San Francisco?*"

"That's where they were the last time I checked,"
Meg replied.

Will still couldn't believe it. "The *San Francisco
Forty Niners?*" he repeated.

Mr. Matthews laughed. "I thought you'd like this
assignment," he said, beaming at Will. "That's why
when Meg said she was going to need help with the
research, I told her you were the man for the job."

Will's jaw dropped. He had no idea what to say.
"Wow, thanks," he managed finally, looking first at
Mr. Matthews, then at Meg. "This is . . . awesome."

"I'm glad you're excited about it," Meg said. "I've
got a few quick phone calls to make, but it should only
take me ten minutes or so. Maybe we can meet in my
office around nine-fifteen? We have to take a commuter flight up, and we're scheduled to leave soon."

"Uh, sure." Will nodded.

"Okay. See you then. Ed will show you the way."

She nodded toward Mr. Matthews, then left, pulling the door closed behind her.

"Wow," Will said again now that he and Mr. Matthews were alone.

"Yeah, I think you'll have a good time with it. And Meg's great—you'll learn a lot from her." He took a seat at his desk and started going through his day planner. "The only problem, of course," he said, glancing up at Will, "is that I don't know how I'm going to top this assignment tomorrow." He chuckled and went back to his work.

Will tried to laugh with him, but he couldn't take his eyes off the closed door. Meg had provided him with the perfect opportunity to talk with Mr. Matthews. He wasn't going to get a better setup than this, and he knew it. But how was he supposed to do it now? He could almost hear the words spilling out: *Gee, Mr. Matthews, thanks for the great assignment and the internship and the extra hours and all the other favors you've done for me. And oh, yeah, by the way—I heard you bribe that U. Michigan scout the other night.*

Will sat down in one of Mr. Matthews's padded brown chairs. The situation was almost laughable. He had decided to confront Mr. Matthews so that he wouldn't feel like a jerk for hiding the truth to protect his own butt, yet here he was totally caving because of the assignment he'd just gotten. But how could he help it? He'd been a Forty Niners fan since he was six years old, and now he was going to get the chance to actually *meet* them. How was he supposed to give that up?

Will glanced over at Mr. Matthews, who had closed his leather-bound day planner and started shuffling papers around on his desk. Every so often he'd make another note on his notepad or crumple something up and throw it across the room into the trash. Will had never seen him miss.

It was really too bad. Mr. Matthews was a good guy, and he'd been so nice to Will. He'd practically treated him like a son. If only he could have waited to see if Ken could have earned the scholarship on his own. *But he didn't,* Will told himself, taking a deep breath. He knew what he had to do.

"Uh—Mr. Matthews?" he said, aware of the slight catch in his voice.

"Yes?" Mr. Matthews answered, looking up from his paperwork.

"I, uh, just thought I should tell you—"

Suddenly Mr. Matthews stood up. "Oh, my goodness, you're right, Will. It's just about time for you to meet up with Meg. I'm glad you noticed—I wasn't watching the clock at all." Immediately he walked to the door and swung it open. "Ready?" he asked, looking back at Will. For a moment Will wasn't sure what to do, but soon enough his body took over.

Slowly he stood from the chair and walked through the door. "Yeah," he answered, starting down the hall.

"So what you're saying," Evan suggested, glancing quickly at Jeremy before returning his gaze to the road, "is that you feel guilty for not moving out to Arizona with your family."

After lunch Jeremy had finally given up his spot behind the wheel to Evan—much to Evan's surprise. He didn't think Jeremy was ever going to loosen up enough to let someone else drive. No wonder Evan and Jessica had never gotten beyond the friendship stage—she obviously preferred guys who were tightly wound.

"That's not what I said," Jeremy insisted, sounding a bit irritated.

"Maybe not exactly, but it's obviously how you feel," Evan replied.

"Well, you're wrong," Jeremy said. "I don't feel guilty—I have nothing to feel guilty about."

"Whatever you say," Evan returned. He wasn't going to push it. He was just trying to make conversation—something Conner hadn't been helping with at all. For nearly seven hours now—four before lunch and two and a half after—Conner had been absolutely silent in the backseat. Even when Evan had tried to engage him, he had just mumbled something moody and incoherent, so instead Evan had been trapped listening to Jeremy rant about everything his parents had to take care of out in Arizona.

By now Evan had learned that Jeremy had two younger sisters—one twelve, one six—who were going to have a hard time with the transition, especially without Jeremy around. He also knew that Mr. Aames wasn't in the best of health, Mrs. Aames was going to be busy helping to run a family business, and Jeremy was feeling incredibly guilty about not being there—even if he wouldn't admit it.

"Okay, so I feel a little guilty," Jeremy said suddenly. "But wouldn't you? I mean—my whole family just relocated, and I'm not going to be around to help them."

"Sure, you are," Evan said. "Isn't that why we're driving out there?"

"Yeah, I guess," Jeremy said. He leaned back in his seat and put his feet up on the dashboard, folding his arms across his chest. Evan glanced over once or twice, contemplating bringing up Jessica or maybe even football—*anything* to get Jeremy to unwind a little, but he decided against it. At least with the silence he was being spared hearing any more of

Jeremy's residual guilt about finishing out his senior year at Big Mesa.

Evan watched as the road signs zipped by. He checked the time on the old watch Jeremy had taped to the dash. *Three-fifteen.* "Hey—Jer," he said with a chuckle. "It looks like we're ahead of schedule."

Evan waited, but there was no response. "Jer," he said again, certain that Jeremy would be thrilled his itinerary had been dead-on so far. "Did you hear what I said?" When Jeremy failed to respond a second time, Evan glanced over, surprised to see Jeremy's head rolling to one side. He had fallen asleep. "Figures," Evan muttered. Just when he'd found something that might cheer Jeremy up.

"Hey—Conner," he tried instead. "What are you doing back there anyway, man? You haven't said a word in over an hour." But once again Evan was greeted by silence. "Oh—you've got to be kidding me," he said to himself. But sure enough, when he shifted the rearview mirror around so he could see the backseat, there was Conner's sleeping form sprawled out behind him.

"Unbelievable," Evan said aloud. It was the middle of the afternoon, and they were on a *road trip!* How could *both* of them possibly be asleep? This was supposed to be an adventure—a chance to cut loose. He glanced at the clock again and chuckled to himself. At least he knew now why they were sticking to

Jeremy's itinerary so well. It was because time only flew when you were having fun.

"This is unbelievable," Evan said again, shaking his head. Between Jeremy's anxious planning and continuous babbling about his family and Conner's moody silences, this trip had been just about as fun as chewing on aluminum foil. They needed something to snap them out of this rut and soon, or they were going to miss out on a prime opportunity for some serious fun.

"Las Vegas," Evan read aloud as he passed yet another road sign. "Via 60 North." It took a minute for the words to sink in, but when they did, Evan's eyes lit up. Immediately he checked the number of miles away on the sign and then started doing the math. *That means we could be there by . . . seven-thirty.*

How could he ignore the karma that had put him behind the wheel at this crucial moment? The road was practically *calling* to him. And a slight detour wouldn't keep them from getting to Jeremy's family by tomorrow evening. He glanced over at Jeremy, who was still fast asleep, then over his shoulder at Conner.

"So what do you say, guys? Should we do Vegas?" Jeremy shifted slightly in his seat and mumbled something that sounded like, "Jessica." In the backseat Conner's mouth dropped open, and he began to snore.

"I'll take that as a yes," Evan said, a wide grin spreading across his face. He turned the wheel ever so slightly and took the exit. Las Vegas was exactly what Evan needed. And it was exactly what Conner and Jeremy needed, whether they wanted to admit it or not.

Jessica Wakefield

Dear Jeremy,

I hope your road trip is going better than mine. We've been on the highway for like eight hours now, and I'm bored out of my mind. I've been trying to get Liz to do something fun with me — like play some kind of travel game or something — but she's busy reading.

I swear she hasn't put that book down since we started out this morning — seriously! — except for lunch and a couple of rest breaks. And every time I try to talk to her, she tells me I should have brought a book — which is totally stupid because she knows I get sick when I read in the car. It's so annoying.

Plus my parents keep switching the radio to that National Public Radio station, so I don't even have any good music to listen to. Just all this talk-radio stuff about news and cars. I can't take it much longer. I really wish I could have driven out to Arizona with you, but I'm sure you're having a good time with Evan. And hopefully Conner's not being too annoying.

Oh, well. I guess I'll go back to memorizing other cars' license plates now. Talk to you soon.

Love,

Jessica

CHAPTER 4

MEANT TO BE

"Ooh! Get some of these," Tia said, pulling a bag of Cheez Doodles from the shelf in the chip aisle.

Andy scrunched up his nose. "I hate those," he said, taking them back out of the cart he and Tia were taking turns pushing through the grocery store.

"But they're *cheesy*," Tia said with a grin. "And I love cheese." She took them from the shelf and tossed them back in the cart.

"Hello? Whose family are we shopping for here?" Andy asked.

"Yours," Tia admitted with a pout, "but with all the time I spend at your house, I would think you'd at least want to have my favorite snack around."

Andy rolled his eyes. "And these are your favorite snack?"

"They're my favorite snack in this aisle," Tia replied, holding back a grin.

"All right," Andy said, "we can get them. But you're going to have to come over tonight and eat some. There's a really cheesy TV movie on at nine—they'd be the perfect thing to eat with it."

"Oh, I'd love to—popcorn," she interrupted herself, pointing across the aisle.

"Thanks," Andy said, snagging a box and crossing one more item off the list Mrs. Marsden had given them.

"But I've got a date," she finished, unable to control the goofy grin that she could feel spreading across her face.

"Oh, yeah," Andy said. "I forgot."

"Andy!" Tia snapped, punching him playfully on the shoulder. "Can't you try to sound at least a little happy for me?"

Andy widened his eyes and forced the fakest smile Tia had ever seen. "Gee, that's great, Tia. You must be so excited."

Tia bit her lip. "Thanks a lot."

"Well—what do you want me to say?" Andy asked.

"I don't know." Tia shrugged. "How about, 'Congratulations'?—bologna." She nodded, prompting Andy to steer the cart toward one of the refrigerated sections. "Or maybe, 'I'm really happy for you,' or something like that."

"What—just because you're hanging out with Angel for a night?" Andy said. He paused, eyeing several different packages of bologna. Finally one seemed to meet his stringent requirements for processed pork product, and he chucked it into the cart and resumed pushing.

"It's not just a night, Andy," Tia corrected him— for like the fiftieth time that day. But for some reason Andy didn't seem to get it. "I told you—I've got a *feeling*."

"Oh, that's right. I forgot. So have you called The Psychic Friends Network yet to see what they think of the whole situation?"

"Very funny, Andy—cereal," Tia said, taking hold of the front of the cart and steering Andy into aisle seven. "But I'm serious. I think we might actually still have something between us—you know, like a spark or something. I mean, it was so weird the way he showed up last night—you know, the timing and everything."

"What, during dinner? Isn't that when everyone always shows up at your house?"

"That's not what I mean," Tia said, running a hand through her dark hair, which was hanging loose around her shoulders today. She'd have to take another shower when she got home and do something with it. "It wasn't just dinnertime," she continued. "It was like two seconds after I'd decided to just bite the bullet and give Trent a call."

Andy raised his eyebrows. "Seriously!" Tia said. "That's why it was so weird! I mean, here I finally decide that I'm going to go for it with this other guy, and then—bam!—Angel shows up on my doorstep. How weird is that?"

"Pretty weird," Andy admitted, grabbing a box of high-fiber twigs and sticks from the top shelf.

"Ee-ew." Tia grimaced. "Who eats those?"

"I'll give you one guess," Andy said with a smile, plunking it into the cart.

"Your dad," Tia said. Andy nodded. "Yeah, mine too—every morning. With raisins. I tried it once, but I couldn't even finish half the bowl before my jaw started to hurt." Andy chuckled, pushing the cart to the end of the aisle, where he automatically turned and headed up the next one.

"So anyway, that's why I think it was fate," Tia said as they passed the canned fruit. "You know—Angel showing up the way he did."

"*Ohhh*," Andy said, nodding.

"I kind of felt like I was in a romantic comedy or something—you know, where the girl thinks she's lost Freddie Prinze Jr. forever, and then he shows up out of the blue with flowers and everything?"

Andy stared down at the floor and shook his head.

"What?" Tia said, suddenly feeling defensive.

He turned his head and glanced at her sideways. "I just don't like to see you getting your hopes up," he said with a shrug. "And I still think you should call Trent."

Tia grabbed the shopping cart and halted it. "What? Why?"

"Because."

Tia scrunched her eyebrows together and stared at him. He wasn't making sense at all.

"Look," Andy said. "I was here the last time Angel left for college, and even if you don't remember what a basket case you were, I do. I just don't think you should set yourself up for that same kind of disappointment all over again."

"Oh Andy," Tia said, standing on her toes and giving him a peck on the cheek. "It's so sweet of you to look out for me, but you don't need to." Andy cocked his head. "Really," Tia insisted. "Things are different this time. For one thing, I've matured."

"Yeah," Andy said, nodding a little too enthusiastically. "I've noticed that. I meant to comment on it back in aisle five when you were conning me into buying you those Cheez Doodles."

Tia shot him a glare. "I mean it," she said as they began to stroll down the aisle again. "I've realized that I don't need a guy constantly by my side to have a good time, and I really think that if things go well tonight and Angel and I decide to get back together, I could handle a long-distance relationship this time around."

Andy inhaled deeply. "You really think you could handle getting back together with Angel and then saying good-bye all over again?" he pressed.

"Yes," Tia replied with confidence. "Especially since it wouldn't be good-bye."

"All right," Andy said. "I won't bug you about it anymore. You want to hand me three packages of those?" he added, pointing to an Oreo display at the end of the row.

"Three?" Tia asked, her eyebrows shooting upward. "Why do you need three bags of them?"

"I'm glad you asked," Andy said as she deposited them into the bottom of the cart. "The first package is to keep me company tonight when I sit down to watch that cheesy TV movie. The second package is to put in the cookie jar so that my mother won't notice that I ate all the first package in one sitting. And the third package is for Friday night."

"What's happening Friday night?" Tia asked.

"I figure that's when you'll realize that Angel has to go back to college soon and start freaking out, so I want to make sure I have plenty of your favorite snack from *this* aisle on hand when you show up at my house to vent your frustration and admit that I was right."

Tia frowned at Andy, but she didn't say a word. She just took the third package of cookies out of the cart and placed them back on the shelf. Then she walked ahead and into the next aisle without even waiting for him to catch up. She definitely wasn't going to need any consolation cookies at the end of the week. It *was* fate that Angel showed up when he did, and when they were still together a month from now, Andy would realize that *Tia* was the one who had been right. Her relationship with Angel was meant to be.

"And there was Cherie, totally psyched because she thought Josh was smiling at her," Gina Cho said, trying to control her giggles, "when the only reason he was even looking in her direction was because she had just walked out of the girls' bathroom and all the way down the hall with a ten-foot trail of toilet paper sticking to her shoe!"

Melissa laughed along with everyone else sitting at the table in House of Java, except for Cherie, who was scowling at all of them.

"Oh, come on, lighten up," Lila said to Cherie.

Melissa smirked. Her friends were sometimes good for some basic entertainment. Today she, Gina, Cherie, Lila, and Amy had spent the day hanging out at the mall, and then—after a pizza at Guido's—they had decided to stop by HOJ and grab some coffee.

All in all, it had been a great day, and Melissa had managed to enjoy herself. But she still would have preferred to spend the time off with Will. Unfortunately, her boyfriend had been at work all day—and it looked like he was going to be there all night too.

He'd called Melissa early that morning to cancel their dinner plans, which was why Melissa had rallied all her friends together for a shopping trip in the first place. He'd been really excited about some assignment involving the San Francisco Forty Niners, which Melissa could understand—Will had been a Forty Niners fan since she had met him. Still, she couldn't help being annoyed that he'd canceled on her. He was already working most of the week. Did he really need to put in more time?

Just then Melissa heard the familiar ringing of the bell above the entrance to House of Java, and when she looked to see who had come in, her mood plummeted. *Perfect,* she thought, looking over Gina's shoulder. *Just what I need right now* . The day had been going so well. Why did Ken and Maria have to show up here and spoil things?

Gina must have seen the look in Melissa's eyes because she stopped giggling and craned her neck toward the door.

"Oh, great," she said, turning back to Melissa

and the rest of the table. "It's Mr. and *Ms.* Perfect."

Cherie, Lila, and Amy all turned to look just in time to see Ken hooking his arm around Maria's shoulders and pulling her close. Maria laughed and pecked him on the cheek, then they both stepped forward to order.

"I'm just about done with my coffee," Gina said, clumsily kicking Cherie under the table.

Cherie coughed and almost spit out a mouthful of latte. "Oh, yeah. Me too. You guys ready to go?" she asked, trying to hide her nearly full mug under the table. Melissa shook her head. It was almost painful to watch her friends when they tried to be sneaky on their own.

"I'm ready," Amy said.

But before anyone could get up to leave, Melissa stopped them. "We're not going anywhere," she said, staring straight ahead. Her friends acting like this was only making it seem like there was a reason she *should* be upset seeing her recent ex back with Maria Slater. She was with Will now anyway, and she wasn't about to give anyone the satisfaction of thinking it mattered to her who Ken dated.

Maria and Ken got their coffees and paid. Once they were done, there was no question about where they were headed. The only empty tables were in the back, near Melissa and her friends, and Melissa wasn't about to vacate the area for them. If Ken wanted to get all cozy and romantic with Maria so soon after he had dumped Melissa, that was fine. She didn't care—but she still wasn't about to make it easy for him.

Melissa felt the hair at the back of her neck stand up as they approached. Maria was flashing that annoyingly huge grin of hers as if she and Ken were the only ones in the room. Well, she was about to realize that they weren't alone.

"You okay, Liss?" Cherie asked as Ken and Maria took a booth just a few feet away. She placed her hand on Melissa's shoulder, but Melissa shrugged it off.

"Of course I'm okay," Melissa hissed. Then in a louder voice she added, "Well, obviously Ken Matthews has decided to go slumming again."

Gina cupped her hand to her mouth and shook with silent laughter as Ken and Maria both whipped their heads around, clearly startled. Cherie smirked.

"Um, I just remembered—I was supposed to be home to walk the dog like an hour ago," Amy said, standing up suddenly. "So I guess I'll just see you all—"

"Speaking of walking dogs," Gina interrupted, staring directly at the back of Maria's head. "I guess Ken had to bring his out for a little fresh air." Melissa smiled, happy to see her friends were as willing as ever to fight her battles so she could sit back and look as cool as she needed to.

"Just let it go," Melissa heard Maria tell Ken. But instead he stood and strode the few feet over to their table. "Back off, Melissa," he said, his six-foot-plus frame towering over her. He completely ignored Gina, even though the comment had come from her.

"Oh, Ken. I'm sorry," she said. "Did something upset you?"

"What's your problem?" Ken snapped. "Don't you and your friends have anything better to do than sit around insulting people?"

Maria came up next to Ken and latched onto his arm. "Really, Ken, you should just ignore her," she urged. She turned to meet Melissa's gaze, her eyes flashing. "She's just upset because you *dumped* her," she added in a voice so loud and clear that anyone in HOJ who had been even remotely listening couldn't have helped but hear her—a thought that made Melissa wince.

Melissa breathed in slowly and forced a cool smile onto her face. "Is that what you think, Maria? That Ken *dumped* me?"

"Yeah, that's right," Maria said, folding her arms across her chest. "Although seeing as how you're completely delusional, I'm sure you have another explanation. Unfortunately, I don't have time to hear it. Come on, Ken. Let's go," she said, tugging at her boyfriend's arm.

"Really?" Melissa pressed, not willing to let her walk away like that. "Because the way I see it, he dumped *you* for *me*. Isn't that right, Ken?"

Maria shook her head, but Ken simply stared at Melissa like he couldn't believe what he was hearing.

"Oh, come on, Ken. You know it's true." Ken opened his mouth to protest, but Melissa kept going. "You were dating plain, boring Maria right up until you got your old spot on the football team back. Then as soon as you were calling the plays again, you got sick of having all your dates at the library. So you dumped Encyclopedia Girl over there and traded up." Melissa bit back a smile as she saw the way Maria's eyes lost a little of their fire.

"Of course, it wasn't long before you started losing your touch and practically losing your games too," Melissa continued. "In fact, if it hadn't been for Will telling you what plays to call, you never would have won the championship. So I can see why with everything else starting to slip away, you'd want to jump back into a *safe* relationship." Melissa nodded toward Maria. "You know, one where you don't really even need a pulse. But don't worry, Ken. I won't hold your weakness against you."

"Bravo, Melissa," Maria said, tilting her head.

"That was great, really, but there's one problem. Nothing *was* slipping away from Ken—he just got sick of you and your stupid mind games. He was *still* the quarterback for SVH, he *still* had the whole team behind him, and to top it off, he got a full scholarship to Michigan for being such an amazing player—or didn't you hear about that?"

A smile crept onto Melissa's face. "Oh, the scholarship. Right," she said. "The one you *earned.*"

"What's that supposed to mean?" Ken demanded, his face getting red.

"Oh, nothing," Melissa said. "I just think it's funny that Maria's defending you with a scholarship that . . . well, that isn't exactly *yours.*"

Maria sighed and tugged at Ken's arm. "Let's just go. We've wasted enough time with her."

"Look, Melissa," Ken said. "I know you think Will deserved that scholarship, and maybe he did—once. But I won it, and you're just going to have to deal with that."

"You didn't *win* that scholarship," Melissa snapped. "Your father *bought* it for you."

"What?" Ken's eyes narrowed to slits. "What are you talking about?"

"Exactly what I said. Well, it wasn't money, but your father did give Hank Krubowski something he wanted, a coaching job—and that's the only reason you'll be playing ball for the Wolverines next year."

"You don't know what—" Ken started, but this time Maria pulled firmly enough on his arm to turn him around.

"Let's just get out of here," she said.

Ken stared at Melissa, his eyes now clouded with confusion. "Yeah, let's go," he agreed, without looking away from Melissa. Finally his expression began to harden again from shock to anger. "I'm not going to listen to one more lie out of your mouth," he told her.

That's just it, Melissa thought, smiling as she watched them leave. *This time I don't have to lie. The truth is so much better.*

"Oh, man, that felt good," Jeremy said, stretching his arms over his head. He breathed in the fresh air streaming through Evan's partially open window and surveyed the scene before him. The sun had all but gone down, its last rays keeping the deep blue sky from turning completely dark, and for the first time all day it felt good to be on the road.

"Welcome back, man," Evan said with a smile.

"Thanks," Jeremy said as he dropped his chin to his chest and rolled his head from side to side. He felt the vertebrae in his neck crack and noticed how tight his shoulder muscles were. *I've got to relax,* he thought, and maybe now that they were finally under way, he could. One thing was certain—the nap had definitely helped.

"How long was I out anyway?" Jeremy asked, reaching for the watch on the dashboard. "Whoa—I was asleep for like four hours!"

"Yeah, you and Conner both," Evan replied, nodding toward the backseat. Jeremy glanced at Conner, who was slouching against the driver's-side door with his legs stretched out across the seat, scribbling in a notebook, but Conner didn't bother to make eye contact. Clearly he wasn't in the mood to talk now any more than he had been all day. *Chipper guy,* Jeremy thought, turning his attention back to Evan and the road.

"So where are we anyway?" he asked, sitting up straight and adjusting his lap belt. He began scanning the highway for road signs so he could check their progress on his map.

"I was wondering when you'd ask," Evan said with a grin. "It's an interesting story, see—"

"That's strange," Jeremy interrupted. "I just saw a sign for the Mojave Desert. That's got to be like three hundred miles away."

"Not exactly," Evan said with a shrug.

"It's kind of odd that there would be a sign way out here—" Jeremy stopped himself midsentence, turning to study Evan's face. "What do you mean, '*not exactly*'?" he asked, and all of a sudden Evan's previous comment came back to him. "And *what's* an interesting story?"

Evan took a quick look at Jeremy—the same grin on his face that had been there before, when Jeremy had asked where they were. Only this time there seemed to be something much more mischievous behind it. A sinking feeling in Jeremy's stomach told him that something had gone wrong, but he didn't know what. And he wasn't sure he wanted to know.

"Okay, now—don't freak out, *but* . . ." Evan's voice—which was mellow to begin with—seemed even slower now.

"Oh my God," Jeremy said as he glimpsed a road sign. "93 North? Aren't we supposed to be on I-10?"

"Well, technically, I guess," Evan answered.

"*Technically?*" Jeremy echoed.

"I mean, according to your itinerary, yes—we're supposed to be on I-10, somewhere near Tucson, I think."

"But . . . we're not. Are we?" Jeremy asked. He was already dreading the answer.

"Nope."

Jeremy felt his shoulders and neck tense up all over again. So much for the nap. "Okay," he said, trying to maintain his cool. "So . . . what happened?"

It was at this point that Conner leaned forward,

taking an interest in the conversation for the first time all day. "What's up?" he asked.

"That's what we're trying to figure out," Jeremy said, keeping his eyes focused on Evan. The last thing he needed right now was Conner's smirk in his face.

"It's simple," Evan said with a carefree smile. "We're going to Vegas."

Jeremy's breath caught in his throat, and he blinked rapidly several times. "We're . . . *what?*"

"Okay, okay, I know it wasn't part of the plan," Evan started, "but when I saw the signs, it was like . . . I don't know—fate or something."

"Fate?" Jeremy asked, hardly able to believe what he was hearing.

"Yeah," Evan said with a shrug. "I just knew it was something we had to do." Jeremy's mouth dropped open, but he couldn't find a word. Conner, on the other hand, appeared social for the first time all day.

"This is classic," he said, sinking back into his seat and practically rocking with silent laughter. It was the first time Jeremy had seen him really smile. And now he realized he preferred the sullen scowl.

"Vegas," Jeremy mumbled, the word sounding all wrong on his lips. This couldn't be happening.

"Yeah, *Vegas,* man," Evan said, slapping the steering wheel a few times to some imaginary beat he seemed to hear inside his head. "It's going to be so cool. We can walk the strip, check out the casinos, go to—"

"We're not going," Jeremy said.

"What do you mean *'we're not going'*? We're almost there," Evan said, gesturing toward a sign. "See? Las Vegas, sixty-two miles."

"I mean, we're not going," Jeremy said. He grabbed his atlas from the floor and opened to the map of California. "We can still get back to Tucson tonight, right? If we just . . ." he trailed off as he realized that they were over three hundred miles away from Tucson now.

A slight chuckle escaped from Evan's throat as he glanced sideways at Jeremy. "You're kidding, right?" Jeremy glared back at him in answer, and Evan furrowed his brow like a confused puppy. "Oh, come on, man!" Evan said. "What's the problem? This is *Vegas* we're talking about. How can you pass that up?"

"Easy," Jeremy said. "Because we're going to Tucson—Las Vegas isn't part of the plan." That was when he heard Conner let out a deep laugh from the backseat. "What? You think this is funny?" Jeremy demanded. "We're hundreds of miles off track now."

Conner just shook his head and went back to scribbling in his notebook, as if Jeremy was only some jerk who was bothering him and not the guy whose car he was riding in and whose road trip he was helping to screw up.

"Hey, man. Chill," Evan said. "It's not that big a deal."

"Not a big deal?" Jeremy shot back. "You decide to hijack my car and head for Las Vegas when I'm supposed to be out in Arizona, helping my family settle in to their new home, and it's not a big deal?"

"Is there anything in your life that *isn't* a big deal?" Conner asked. Jeremy whirled to face him, but he hadn't even bothered to look up from his writing.

"Seriously, Jer," Evan said, causing Jeremy to return his focus up front. "Just listen for a second." Jeremy gritted his teeth. The last thing he wanted to do was to listen to any more of Evan's idiotic logic. But short of yanking away the steering wheel, what else was he going to do?

"Here we are—three seventeen-year-old guys on a road trip. *A road trip,* Jer," he repeated, drawing the words out. "The ultimate coming-of-age experience." Jeremy caught a glimpse in the rearview mirror of Conner grinning in the backseat, but he tried to ignore it. "Now, we could just drive straight out to Tucson, help your family, and drive straight back, but where would the adventure be? What kind of story would that make? *Or*"—and here he paused to shoot Jeremy a sly grin—"we could go to Vegas. Just a quick side trip, of course—and we could still be in Tucson by tomorrow night—but it's *Vegas*. The bright lights, the big city, the legendary strip. Casinos, Elvis impersonators, cheesy entertainment. Wedding chapels on one side of the street, divorce courts on the other. It's a total fantasy world—like Disneyland for adults. And we're sure to come out with at least one good story, maybe two." Jeremy cocked his head, considering everything Evan had said. "But if you just want to turn around and head for Tucson . . . well, hey—that's okay too," Evan said, raising one shoulder, as if it really made no difference at all which one Jeremy chose.

"I don't know," Jeremy began, the two options weighing heavily on his mind. Las Vegas did sound like a lot of fun, and he had always wanted to go there. And it did seem kind of foolish to turn around now, when they were so close. But still . . . his family was counting on him. "Do you really think we could still make Tucson by tomorrow night?"

"Sure," Evan said. "It can't be more than . . . what? Four hundred miles away? So with three of us to drive . . ."

"It would take us about eight hours." Jeremy nodded, consulting the map. Evan was right—it was doable. And they could probably even still make his family's house in time for dinner.

Then, for reasons he wasn't quite certain of, Jeremy turned to the backseat. "What do you think, Conner?" he asked.

Conner stopped writing and looked up. "Your car, your call," he said with a shrug and not the slightest trace of his trademark smirk. It was the first serious—and even somewhat respectful—remark he'd made to Jeremy.

"Okay," Jeremy said, staring at the road stretching out before them. He took a deep breath, the uneasiness in his gut telling him he was probably going to regret his next words. "Vegas it is."

Elizabeth Wakefield

Okay, so here's what I don't get—how can identical twins—two people who developed from the same egg with all the same genes and all the same DNA—be soooooo different? I love Jessica. Really, I do. But long car trips with her are a nightmare! She's so fidgety, and she keeps trying to get me to play stupid travel games to pass time—like finding things along the side of the road that start with all the letters of the alphabet—stuff we used to do when we were six years old. Plus every time a decent song comes on the radio, she has to sing along with it. It's no wonder Mom and Dad keep changing the station back to public radio. At least Jessica doesn't know all the words to <u>Car Talk</u>.

Conner McDermott

Disneyland for adults, huh? I guess I can see that. What I can't see is "Mr. Itinerary" up there loosening up enough to actually enjoy it.

Then again, I'm not sure how much I should loosen up once we get there. It may seem like Disneyland to Evan, but I can tell you—when Mickey Mouse starts serving up free drinks to keep you in the casino, I'll bet all the alcoholics in the room start to get a little itchy.

Viva Las Vegas

"I just can't believe her," Ken said, bringing his car to a stop just behind Mrs. Slater's silver Volvo wagon.

"And you're right not to," Maria jumped in.

"No—I mean I can't believe her *nerve*," Ken explained. "What does she do anyway? Just sit around all day thinking of new ways to torment people?"

"Probably," Maria answered. "And it looks like you're her latest target."

"Yeah, well, you're obviously at the top of her list too," Ken said, feeling more than a small twinge of guilt. "I'm—I'm sorry about that," he muttered, avoiding Maria's gaze. He tried to avoid talking about Melissa at all, but he knew Maria had to wonder how he ever could have dated such an obnoxious person. The truth was, he could barely believe he'd done it too.

"It's no big deal," Maria said with a shrug. "She doesn't get to me."

Ken frowned, realizing that Maria really seemed to mean it. "How do you do that?" he asked.

"Do what?"

"Just ignore her."

Maria exhaled sharply. "It's easy—nothing she says is true."

Ken shook his head, amazed at how easily Maria dismissed Melissa's comments. But then, the things Melissa had said about Maria had just been immature insults. What she'd said about Mr. Matthews bribing Hank Krubowski, though . . . he couldn't seem to let go of it. The worst part was that he couldn't trust his own father enough to know for a fact that it was a lie. But it had to be, right? It was so crazy, it couldn't be true.

"All I know," Maria continued, "is that you shouldn't waste another minute thinking about Melissa or any of the stupid things she says. She's just upset because *you* dumped her and *I* won the Senate scholarship, and once she's done with us, she'll start attacking someone else for an equally bizarre reason. She's *completely* psychotic. So will you please forget about her?"

"Okay, okay," Ken said, his eyebrows shooting up at the passion in Maria's tone. "I won't bring her up again."

Maria giggled. "Sorry," she said. "I just can't stand her. And you know there aren't many people I'd talk about that way," she added.

Ken nodded. It was true. Maria was one of the most open-minded people he knew—she hated to see anyone treated unfairly. But Melissa had pushed her one step too far. Come to think of it, Melissa had pushed a lot of people one step too far, and now she was trying to do it to him.

"It's fine," Ken told her. "You're right. I shouldn't waste my time thinking about it."

"Good," Maria said, opening her door to get out. "I'm glad to hear you say that, because she's so not worth it." She stood, adjusting her feet in their chunky black sandals. Then, bending gracefully and balancing one knee on the passenger seat, she leaned back in to kiss him. "Call me tomorrow?" she asked. Ken nodded. "Okay—I'll see you later."

He watched as she walked quickly up the driveway, her brightly colored crocheted bag bouncing at her side. When she reached the front porch, she turned around to wave, and Ken flicked his lights on and off twice to let her know he'd seen her.

Man, he was lucky to have Maria back. It sure was nice to be free of Melissa and all of her wacko head games. Unfortunately, breaking up with her obviously hadn't taken him completely out of her manipulation range, and this thing about the scholarship . . . it was really out there.

Of course, it didn't help that Hank Krubowski

had handed him the scholarship right after he'd bombed the championship game. *If I could just get some kind of guarantee that I earned it on my own,* Ken thought. Then he could really forget about what Melissa had said.

It wasn't until Ken had backed out of the driveway and started to head home that it hit him. There *was* a way he could get a guarantee. All he had to do was confront the one person who knew the truth—his dad.

"You're not going to win, you know," Tia scolded her hair in the bathroom mirror. "In the end you'll do what I want you to do, or I'm just going to pin you up!" She flicked the curling iron on high and leaned closer to the mirror, wiping away a smudge of lipstick while she waited.

"Who are you talking to?"

Tia jumped, startled by her mother's voice. "Oh," she gasped, "you surprised me."

Her mother peeked into the bathroom and checked behind the door. "Are you alone in here?" she asked.

Tia snorted. "Yeah, I was just talking to my stupid hair," she said, holding out the disobedient piece with a scowl.

"Here," her mother said, setting down the freshly

folded towels she had just taken out of the dryer. She held Tia's face gently between both of her hands and examined the situation. Then, as if she were an experienced hairdresser and not part owner of a deli, she picked up the curling iron and expertly twirled the strand around it. Tia smiled, comforted by her mother's touch and glad to have someone else wrestling with her thick hair for a while.

Mrs. Ramirez slowly released Tia's hair from the iron, then fluffed it a little with both hands. Next she picked up the cute butterfly clip on the sink's edge and pinned one side of Tia's hair back from her face. Tia glanced in the mirror—the effect was exactly what she had been hoping for.

"Thanks, Mom," she said gratefully.

Mrs. Ramirez smiled and kissed her forehead. "You're beautiful," she said. "You and Angel have a good time tonight." Then she picked up the towels and continued down the hall to the linen closet. Tia grinned. Sometimes her mom was so cool. And the best part was that unlike Andy, who'd been telling her not to jump back into things too quickly all day, her mother had completely reserved judgment. She hadn't expressed any sort of excitement at the prospect of Tia and Angel getting back together, and she also hadn't issued any warnings. Andy could definitely take a lesson from her.

Tia was just beginning to feel calm about the whole situation when the doorbell rang. "Oh my God," she whispered, checking herself over in the mirror once again. She adjusted the wide straps of her bright pink, silk camisole dress, and pressed her lips together to blot her lipstick. Then, slipping her bare feet into a pair of suede mules, she made her way down the hall to the door.

"Hey," she said, grinning as she greeted Angel in the foyer. Her little brother Tomás had already let him in, and Angel was now crouched down, accepting a big hug from the six-year-old.

Tia giggled. It was nice to see that Tomás's affection for her former boyfriend hadn't changed over the last three months. But then, Angel really had been like an adopted big brother—to all three of Tia's younger siblings.

"Angel, good to see you," Mrs. Ramirez said, rounding the corner. She too stepped forward and gave him a brief hug and a peck on the cheek. "How's school?"

"Great," Angel said with a nod, "although it's always nice to come home."

"Bless you for saying so," Mrs. Ramirez said. "We hope Tia feels the same way next year around this time," she added, glancing at her daughter.

"Come on, Mom." Tia groaned, rolling her eyes. "Of

course I will—there's no way a college cafeteria is ever going to compare to the meals you and Dad make."

"I can vouch for that," Angel agreed, and the three of them all laughed.

"Okay, Tomás," Mrs. Ramirez said, taking her youngest child by the hand. "Speaking of dinner, why don't you come help me in the kitchen?" It was obvious that Tomás wanted to stay and play with Angel, but reluctantly he accompanied his mother out of the hallway, leaving Tia and Angel alone.

"You look"—Angel paused, smiling as he scanned Tia from head to toe—"*amazing*." As unusual as it was for Tia to feel shy, she felt her cheeks heat up with a blush.

"Thanks," she said. "So do you." Angel was wearing a crisp white shirt that set off his dark skin perfectly, with a pair of khaki pants he must have picked up since he started college. Tia had never seen them before, and there was a time when she could have drawn pictures of every item of clothing Angel owned.

"Ready to go?" Angel asked, opening the door and holding it for her. Tia nodded and walked past him, grabbing her jacket on the way out. Angel followed close behind her down the front steps and walked beside her as they headed down the brick walkway that led to the side of the road where he had parked his car.

91

They were halfway down the walk when Tia instinctively reached for him and looped her arm around his. "Oh, I'm sorry," she said when she realized what she'd done. "It's just—um, a habit, I guess." She started to pull her arm away, but he caught her hand in his and gave it a gentle squeeze.

"It's all right," he said, and instead of dropping her hand, he held on to it all the way to the car—right up until he opened the door for her.

Tia felt a wave of excitement run through her body, and she shivered despite the warm night air. Angel smiled at her as she slid into the passenger seat, and when he closed the door for her, she knew what Angel had said was true.

It *was* all right. In fact, everything was going to be just fine.

"Wow. I mean—wow."

It was just about all Jeremy could manage when faced with all the lights. Red, purple, gold, blue, green. It was like someone had bought every last strand of Christmas lights in the world and dropped them in a heap in the middle of the desert.

"You're not kidding," Evan agreed. He was sitting in the backseat now, but the way he was craning his neck and leaning forward between Jeremy and Conner, he might as well have been in the front.

"Take a right up there," Evan told Conner, pointing toward the next intersection up ahead. "Then we can get right onto the strip." Jeremy didn't bother to argue, even though he was riding shotgun and therefore supposed to be the navigator. He was so distracted by the garish scenery that he was kind of glad Evan was taking charge.

"Up here?" Conner asked.

"Yeah, this one," Evan said, pointing at the road on the right.

"Tropicana Avenue," Conner read aloud. "Man, even the street names sound fake."

"I know," Evan said, his voice practically shaking with excitement. "Isn't it great?"

Jeremy wasn't so sure. He glanced up at the evening sky, which should have been dark blue by now, and marveled at the way it glowed pink. *I thought New York was the city that never slept,* he thought. But instead of feeling excited, as Evan obviously was, Jeremy had actually begun to grow a little nervous. He had a sudden urge to reach around the car and make sure all the doors were locked, and he would have if he'd been alone. But he didn't want to look like too much of an idiot in front of Conner and Evan.

Just then Conner turned to him and snorted. "Are you going to make it?" he asked sarcastically, obviously noticing the shock in Jeremy's expression. But Jeremy didn't have to come up with a flip answer for Conner because two seconds later, when Conner turned back to the road, Jeremy saw his jaw drop too.

"Whoa," Conner said under his breath. The turn Evan had instructed them to take had brought them directly to the strip. On their right was a hotel that seemed more like a medieval castle, complete with bright pink spires and glowing towers. On the left another hotel looked like it had been airlifted right out of New York City. It had a facade with the New York skyline that included the Statue of Liberty and even the Brooklyn Bridge. "This place is wacked," Conner muttered.

"Surreal," Evan said.

More like insane, Jeremy thought, wondering why he had ever agreed to come. A red light at the intersection gave him the opportunity to check out two more hotels across the street—the MGM Grand, which was huge and, according to its City of Entertainment sign, included a theme park, entertainment, and thirty restaurants, and the Tropicana, a slightly smaller place—although small was obviously a relative term in Las Vegas—and obviously the one for which the street had been named.

"Which way?" Conner asked just before the light turned green.

"Right," Jeremy said, eyeing the seemingly endless expanse of unnatural color to his left. Somehow turning away from what appeared to be the heart of the strip seemed safer. He heard Evan sigh.

"Actually, you're right," Evan said after a moment, his grin returning. "This is better. We can go all the way to this end of the strip and then loop around and drive the whole thing!"

"I don't know," Jeremy said, his stomach tightening. "I think maybe we should just try to find a reasonable place to stay and call it a night." He caught Conner's eye roll but chose to ignore it. He was beginning to get used to the nonstop attitude. "We're going to have to be on the road early tomorrow to make up for lost time. Plus I really want to call my family and see how they're doing before it gets too late. Trisha goes to bed at eight o'clock."

It seemed obvious from the way Conner shook his head that he thought Jeremy was pretty lame, but Evan nodded slowly, as if mulling things over, then smiled.

"Okay," he said with a shrug. "Sure. Let's find a room first and put our stuff away. Then you can call your parents." Jeremy relaxed a little, letting himself breathe. "Besides, we'll have plenty of time to explore later," Evan added. Jeremy winced, but he managed to keep quiet. *One thing at a time,* he told himself, holding out hope that even Evan would opt for a quick bite to eat and a good night's sleep once they got settled in a room and realized how tired they all were.

"How about this place?" Conner asked as he turned into the last big hotel at the end of the strip. It was a huge, curved, white building with lots of palm trees out front.

"Yeah," Jeremy said, sizing it up. "I like this one. It looks . . . quiet."

"I'm not sure quiet exists here," Conner said, but he pulled the Mercedes into a parking space. Jeremy stepped out of the car slowly, his body cramped from riding for so long.

"Ahhh . . . it feels good to stretch," Evan said as he climbed out. He propped one of his legs on the hood and bent over it. Jeremy cringed, still conditioned to treat the car like an antique from years of watching his father lovingly restore it, but once again he bit his tongue. He'd come to the conclusion that the quicker they could get in and out of Vegas, the better off they'd be, which meant he was going to have to pick his battles.

Evan repeated the same stretch with the other leg, then hopped up and down a few times, letting his arms hang loosely at his sides. "Okay. Let's go!" he said, and together they headed in.

Once they were in the lobby, Jeremy felt himself beginning to relax again. The place was obviously expensive but not too over the top. It could have been a hotel anywhere—and somehow the thought of being someplace other than Vegas right now was comforting.

As they approached the customer-service desk, Jeremy stepped forward a bit, taking the lead. "Hi. We'd like a room, please," he said, gesturing to himself, Conner, and Evan as if the people working behind the counter might not be able to figure out that the three of them were together.

"I see," a blond woman in a white blouse said, smiling politely. She glanced at all three of them, but her eyes lingered on Evan the longest. She was clearly put off by his disheveled appearance—a Pearl Jam T-shirt that had seen better days and shoulder-length black hair that was in full shag mode from being blown around in the car all day. But at least she didn't question their age. Obviously they all looked old enough to be there on their own.

She tapped a computer keyboard lightly with her long, pink fingernails. "We do have a few rooms with two queen-size beds available," she told Jeremy. "Will you be needing a cot?"

"Yeah, that would be great. Thanks," Jeremy said, surprised—and thankful—at how easily things seemed to be going. The woman had seemed a little rude at first, but maybe she'd had a long day.

"I just need you to fill out this information here," the woman, whose name tag indicated that her name was Nancy, told him. She thrust a white postcard and a heavy silver pen in front of him. "And that will be . . . two hundred and ninety-nine dollars. How would you like to pay?"

Jeremy coughed, and his voice caught in his throat. "Uh—with someone else's credit card?" he suggested weakly. Nancy pressed her lips together and smiled her polite smile again, but she obviously was not amused. "Um, is that . . . your regular rate?" Jeremy asked after a moment of awkward silence.

"It varies," Nancy said, "but we do have a convention going on this week, so I'm afraid room availability is quite limited. Would you like to take the room?"

Jeremy turned to Evan and Conner, but he didn't bother to ask. Even if they hadn't looked completely shell-shocked, Jeremy knew he couldn't afford his portion of that bill. "No, I don't think so. But thanks anyway," he said, and the three of them walked out to the car in virtual silence.

"Three hundred bucks!" Jeremy said once they were all back in the car. "I hope all the rooms around here aren't that expensive."

"Don't sweat it," Evan said with a wave of his hand. "This place is packed with hotels. I'm sure we can find something cheap." But instead of being reassured by what he had previously seen as Evan's calm manner, this time Jeremy was a bit irritated. Did the guy have to be so nonchalant about *everything?*

And just as Jeremy had feared, the prices weren't much better at the next two places. First they checked out a pyramid-shaped hotel with a sphinx out front, where rooms went for two hundred thirty a night—because it was a big vacation week, the desk clerk said.

The third hotel they tried was the castle-shaped building Jeremy had spotted on their way in, which was a little better at one sixty-nine but still out of their price range.

"This is ridiculous," Evan said when they hopped back in the car for the third time. "These hotels offer discounts all the time—they're just not offering them to us, and you know why? *Ageism.*"

Conner laughed, but Jeremy wasn't in the mood for any more of Evan's philosophizing. He just wanted to get a room and call his family, who by this time were probably worried sick that he hadn't been in touch after an entire day of driving.

"Are you sure it's not *hair*-ism?" Conner asked. "Because every time someone sees us coming, the first thing they're checking out is that shrub on your head you call a haircut."

"Very funny," Evan acknowledged, "but no—I don't think it has anything to do with my hair—except for the fact that it's not gray, and I'm not fifty-five with a nice suit and money falling out of my pockets. I'm telling you, these people are being rude and quoting high room rates to us because we're young—they think we'll be trouble, and they know we're not going to drop a thousand dollars in their casinos."

Jeremy exhaled noisily, but Evan didn't seem to notice.

"Personally, I think we should demand to speak to a manager if this happens at the next place," he continued. "I don't think we should just sit back and let all of them judge us because of the way we look. I mean, come on—do they really think we're completely irresponsible just because we're a little younger than their average customers? We have just as much right to stay here as anyone else."

"Yeah," Conner agreed with an exaggerated nod. "Maybe you should explain to them that you're just here to cut loose and go crazy."

"Nice," Evan returned. "Use my own words against me. But I still say we should ask to see a manager if—"

"We're not going to talk to any managers," Jeremy interrupted, feeling like he was ready to explode.

"We're going to drive a little farther down the strip—away from all these high-priced places—and see if we can find something we can afford. Even if it's not on the strip," he added, glaring at Evan.

He half expected an argument, but clearly his commanding tone had shocked them into obedience finally. Good. It was about time Conner—and especially Evan—realized this wasn't just some kind of game. He needed to get to Arizona to help his family, and they'd already wasted enough time with Evan's little detour.

"There," Jeremy said, pointing to what appeared to him to be one of the cheesiest places they'd seen yet. It looked old too, like it had been there a lot longer than the posh hotels they'd tried so far. "That looks like something we can afford." There was no argument from the backseat, so Conner just pulled in, and they tried again.

"How much for a room for the night?" Jeremy asked as soon as they'd made it to the front desk.

"For the three of you?" the woman behind the counter asked. Jeremy nodded. "Sixty-nine."

"We'll take it," Jeremy said. He filled out the required paperwork quickly, using the credit card his parents had given him for necessities, and took the key the old lady had placed on the counter.

"Number one forty-two," the woman said, her

raspy voice and yellowing teeth branding her as a lifetime smoker. "Down the hall, take a left, and go all the way to the end. Casino's on the strip side," she added, eyeing all three of them, "coffee shop's open seven to eleven, with five-cent coffee and twenty-five-cent doughnuts, and there's a deli and a diner just off to the left of the cashier's cage out front. Enjoy your stay."

When she finished rattling off the instructions she'd obviously given countless times before, she turned and retreated into the office, leaving Jeremy, Evan, and Conner alone.

"To the room?" Jeremy asked. Evan and Conner nodded their agreement.

The red-carpeted hallway was flecked with bits of yellow that had probably been brighter and a bit more golden about ten years ago, but overall, the place was relatively clean. Not spotless—but passable. Especially for three teenagers who were just passing through.

When they reached number one forty-two, Jeremy shoved the key in the lock, fidgeted with it a bit, and finally swung open the door to reveal a small room with two double beds, a narrow bureau with a television, and a large window flanked by red-and-gold curtains that matched the bedspreads. The cot they'd asked for was supposed to arrive a little later.

"Cool," Evan said, flopping down on one of the beds. His peppy mood seemed to have been restored, even if he was acting at least a little more subdued now. Conner nodded and started walking around, opening drawers and checking out the bathroom, but Jeremy had just one thing on his mind. He pulled out his wallet and unfolded the piece of paper where he had scrawled his relatives' address—the place where his family was staying for a couple of days while they moved all their stuff into their new home.

He read the instructions on the room phone, dialed nine like it said, and then punched in the phone number. *They're probably going out of their minds,* he thought, listening to the ringing tone and anxiously anticipating hearing his mom, his dad, and even his sisters' voices. But the ringing didn't stop. He let it go for thirteen rings, then fourteen, and finally gave up when it reached twenty. Slowly he replaced the receiver in its cradle and slouched forward.

"No answer?" Conner asked. Jeremy was surprised. He didn't think Conner had even been paying attention.

"No," he said. "I don't get it. It's eight-thirty. Where could they be?" Irrational thoughts streamed through his mind—they'd been in a car accident; they'd been robbed and were all down at the police station filling out reports. And of course the clincher: his father had had another heart attack, and everyone was at the hospital.

"They're probably just out to dinner—celebrating the move," Evan suggested, which Jeremy knew was probably a more likely explanation than anything he'd come up with. But still, he couldn't help worrying—and he really couldn't stop beating himself up for continuing north on Evan's crazy whim instead of turning back and heading in the right direction. For one insane moment he'd been tempted at the idea of seeing Las Vegas, but deep down he'd known this whole Las Vegas trip was a big mistake, and he should have listened to himself.

Maria Slater

Magazines are always having those quizzes like "What Kind of Girlfriend Are You?" or "What's Your Flirting Style?" And once you've answered all the questions and totaled up your score, you get lumped into a category with a funky title like "Daring Diva" or "Radical Romantic." But there's always some reason why it's good to be any of the options, and they never say anything to make anyone look too bad.

So what I'd like to see is a write-up that would apply to Melissa Fox. Because no matter how hard I look, I can't seem to find any of her positive qualities. Personally, I think she belongs in a category like "<u>Manipulative Mama:</u> You know what you want and you'll do anything to get it—now, if you could just get a life." Or maybe "<u>Villainous Vixen:</u> Lying, cheating, and stealing are your specialties. Consider incorporating prison orange into your wardrobe now so it won't come as such a shock later."

Hey—I'm pretty good at this. Maybe I should talk to Liz about creating a new feature for the <u>Oracle</u>. . . .

CHAPTER

Insider's Tour

6

Conner took a long sip of his coffee and gazed around the diner where he, Evan, and Jeremy had come to unwind once they'd gotten all their stuff into the room.

It was straight out of the fifties—a U-shaped counter with spinning chrome-and-vinyl stools, orange padded booths against the wall, and a big black-and-white-checkered dance floor with a small stage at one end and a jukebox at the other. Conner had to smile. It wasn't exactly an atmosphere that encouraged drinking—in fact, it was probably the least glitzy place in Las Vegas.

"Hey—did you get a look in the casino when we walked by?" Evan asked, spinning around once on his bar stool.

"Yeah," Jeremy said, picking up his big, white mug and taking a sip of the decaf coffee he had ordered. "It looked kind of gloomy—sort of like a cave."

"They're all like that," a woman who was sitting

two stools down from Evan said. She smiled at them, and Conner noticed she wasn't too much older than them—probably barely twenty-one herself. She was pretty too, with very piercing green eyes.

"But that doesn't make sense," Evan said, leaning over toward the girl. "If they want to attract people, shouldn't they make the casinos brighter and happier?"

She shook her head. "Not really. I mean, some of them are pretty nice—they don't all feel quite as dark as a cave," she added, glancing at Jeremy. "But you'll notice that none of them have windows or any natural light—or clocks, for that matter. That's because they don't want you to know what time it is."

"Why not?" Evan asked, tilting his head to the side.

"So you won't think twice about having another drink and gambling a little longer," she explained.

Evan nodded. "I hadn't thought of that, but it makes sense. And they don't ever close down either, do they?"

"Some do, but not many. So you could go in there at nine A.M. and see people who are still dressed in last night's cocktail dresses and suits, throwing back margaritas and shooting craps like the night is still young." She smiled at them and raised her perfectly arched eyebrows. "It's kind of creepy. I'm Laney, by the way," she added, extending her arm. Evan grasped her hand and shook it.

"I'm Evan," he said, "and this is Jeremy, and that's Conner."

"Nice to meet you," she said.

"You too," Jeremy responded, but Conner just nodded. She seemed like an intelligent person, and she seemed to know Vegas pretty well too. He wondered if maybe she lived here. Did anyone actually live in Vegas? He was about to ask, but Evan beat him to it.

"So, are you on vacation here, or—"

"Actually, I live in North Vegas, not too far away," she said. "Where are you guys from?"

"We're from California," Evan answered. "Sweet Valley—it's not too far from Los Angeles."

"Yeah? So what are you doing here?"

"We're on our way to visit his family in Tucson," Evan said, nodding toward Jeremy.

Laney looked confused. "Tucson? Isn't this a little out of your way?"

"Yes," Jeremy blurted, glaring at Evan, who simply shrugged.

"We took a little detour," Evan explained, shifting on the bar stool. "We'll get back on track tomorrow."

"*Tomorrow?*" Laney said. "You mean you're spending only one night in Vegas?" Conner watched with amusement as Evan glanced at Jeremy before he answered. As if Mr. Itinerary was going to budge about leaving first thing in the morning.

"Yeah," Evan said, a hint of disappointment in his voice. He shot another look at Jeremy, but Jeremy was carefully avoiding eye contact with both of them.

"One night, wow," Laney repeated, shaking her head so that her short, black hair swished at her neckline. "Then you definitely need the insider tour."

Evan's face lit up instantly. "The insider tour?"

"Absolutely," Laney responded. She pulled a few dollars out of her purse and set them on the counter next to her mug. "I'm going to show you around this city from a local's point of view."

"Excellent!" Evan said, hopping off his bar stool. "Let's go."

"Anyone else?" Laney asked.

Conner thought about it, but he didn't really feel like going on a sight-seeing tour. Especially when most of the sights would probably involve booze. "Nah, that's okay," he said.

"How about you, Jer?" Evan asked, punching him playfully on the shoulder. Jeremy winced, but Evan didn't even notice. He was bouncing around like an excited Chihuahua.

"No, thanks. I think I'm just going to grab a bite to eat here and call it a night. We have to be on the road early, you know," he reminded Evan.

"I know, Dad—don't worry. I won't stay out too late," Evan teased, but Jeremy didn't even crack a smile. Just then their waitress came by with the coffeepot.

"Would you like a warm-up?" she asked.

"Yeah, thanks," Conner said, pushing his mug forward, but Jeremy held up his hand.

"Decaf for me," he said.

"Oh, that's right," the waitress said, exchanging a wry smile with Laney. Conner hadn't noticed before, but they obviously knew each other. And now that he took a second look at the waitress, whose face he hadn't really paid much attention to, he realized that she was pretty young too—maybe early twenties.

"Hey, Maggie, I'm going to show Evan here around town," Laney said. "I've got my cell phone if Jeremy or Conner needs to get in touch with him. You have the number, right?"

"I sure do," Maggie responded.

"Okay, then," Laney said, "we'll see you guys later."

"See ya!" Evan practically shouted as he and Laney walked out the door.

Jeremy stared after them, shaking his head. "I can't believe he just did that," he muttered.

"What?" Conner asked.

"Walked out of here with a complete stranger in the middle of a strange city when we have to be on the road early in the morning."

Conner shrugged. "That's Evan," he said, and as he looked around the diner with all of its bizarre fifties decorations, he decided it was about time he had a change of scenery too. This place reminded him too much of the weirdo fifties diner in Sweet Valley that he and Alanna had gone to on their first postrehab date—and Alanna was one of the things he was trying to forget about right now. He took a dollar out of his pocket and set it on the counter.

"What are you doing?" Jeremy asked.

"Taking off for a while," Conner said.

"To do what?"

"Look around," Conner said, turning to go. He heard Jeremy sigh from behind him and rolled his eyes. No wonder Elizabeth's twin was dating him— he was just as uptight as she was.

"Just remember to be back here early," Jeremy called after him. "We've—"

"I know," Conner said over his shoulder. "We've got to be on the road early in the morning."

It was kind of funny. For a while Conner had actually thought hanging with Jeremy might be a good idea. He was such a straight arrow, there was no way he'd ever encourage Conner to have a drink. But now Conner was glad to be walking away. A few more minutes with Mr. Itinerary just might drive him to it.

"And the part where she thought he was dead just because she found his hat on the beach—was that stupid or what?" Tia widened her eyes at Angel over the top of the hurricane glass that surrounded a tall, white pillar candle in the center of their table.

"Yeah, I don't think they put much thought into that part," Angel agreed.

"I don't think they put much thought into *any* of the movie," Tia said. "It was so bad."

"Yeah, I know," Angel said with a chuckle. He looked at her, holding her gaze with his gorgeous dark eyes. "So then why did I have such a good time?"

Tia felt a shiver run through her entire body from head to toe. "Me too," she said, feeling shy for the second time that night. "I guess it's—um, the company."

"Definitely," Angel agreed. He reached for a nacho from the pile they had ordered layered with chili, four kinds of cheese, hot peppers, guacamole, and sour cream. "Boy, I've missed these at college," he said, plunking a whole chip into his mouth.

"What—no nachos at Stanford?" Tia teased.

"They've got 'em," Angel admitted, "and there are even some decent Tex-Mex restaurants around, but nothing compares to these. Except maybe the ones we used to make at your house."

Tia giggled at the memory. She and Angel had spent endless hours in the Ramirez kitchen over the years making their homemade nachos, then cuddling up to watch a movie on the sofa together afterward. "Yeah, that was one of my favorite ways to spend a Saturday night," she agreed. "That and—"

"Are you ready to rumble!" Angel interrupted.

"Yes!" Tia said. "I can't believe you remember that."

"How could I forget? Not many guys are lucky enough to have a girlfriend who can get into WWF wrestling."

"Don't forget," Tia reminded him, "that phase only lasted for about a year—then we both got kind of sick of it."

"Yeah, but it was fun for a while," Angel said. "Especially when you used to try to practice the pile driver on me."

"Only I could never lift you more than two inches off the floor," Tia added with another giggle. Angel started laughing too, and Tia joined him.

"We really had a lot of fun," Tia said once she'd recovered from the laughing fit. She placed her hand on the table and leaned forward slightly, staring into

Angel's eyes and remembering how she used to get lost in them for minutes at a time. And when she felt Angel's hand on top of hers, she realized it had happened again.

"We still do," he said, gazing back at her intently. Tia felt her heart lurch, and for a moment she thought it might have jumped straight into her throat. Angel must have felt her stiffen slightly because he took his hand away and started picking at the nachos again. Tia reached for another chip herself, not knowing exactly what to say, but even as she started eating, her hand continued to tingle as if Angel were still holding on to it. And that was when Tia realized that the old electricity between her and Angel was still there, and it was still as powerful as ever.

In fact, as she watched him across the table, she realized with satisfaction how easy it had been for them to pick up where they had left off. It was almost as if they'd never been apart.

I probably should have stayed home, Ken thought as he rode the elevator up to the fifth floor of the *Tribune* building. He'd waited at home for his dad for nearly two hours before he got sick of waiting and decided to come find him at work.

The stainless-steel doors opened onto the floor,

and Ken paused before stepping out. His father hated to be bothered at the paper. But this was important.

He made his way down the hall past numerous cubicles, the break room, the water cooler, and finally to the back part of the floor, where his father's office was. And it looked like he was in luck. The lights were on, and his dad was in his chair—back to Ken—with his feet propped on the windowsill.

The door was half shut, but Ken didn't bother to knock—he just pushed it open. "Dad, I need to—" He stopped suddenly as the person in the chair spun around and he saw it wasn't his father. "Will?"

"Uh, yeah, your dad's still out covering a basketball game," Will responded, sitting up awkwardly.

"What are you doing here so late?" Ken asked.

"Oh, your dad sent me out to see the Forty Niners today," Will explained. "I just got back a little while ago from the commuter flight, and I wanted to write up some copy from the interviews I helped with today while it's all, you know, fresh in my mind. Plus I wanted to run it past your dad, and I figured he'd be back pretty soon." He stopped, his expression suddenly uneasy. "You can, um, hang out and wait for him too if you want," he offered, gesturing toward the chairs. "I don't . . . mind or anything."

It was pretty weird that the two of them had gone

from enemies to two guys who could sit in a room together waiting for a man that was now involved in both of their lives. Then again, the problem had never been between them, exactly. It was about Melissa.

And Will deserves to know what his girlfriend's up to, Ken thought. He was the one who had gotten them back together. He'd been convinced that doing it would somehow make up for whatever his role was in their split. But now he wasn't so sure he'd done Will a favor.

"No, thanks." Ken shook his head. "What I wanted to talk to him about is . . . personal." He shoved his hand through his hair. "But I guess it kind of is something you should know," he added.

Will frowned. "What—is something wrong?" he asked, resting his elbows on Mr. Matthews's desk.

"Well . . . it's just that Melissa pulled one of her stunts today," Ken admitted. He kicked at the grungy carpeting, avoiding Will's gaze. "And I think you should know what she said."

Will's eyes narrowed. "What did she say?" he asked, his voice sounding a little strange.

Ken took a deep breath, then let it out all at once. "She's telling people that my dad bribed Hank Krubowski to get me the scholarship," he blurted.

Ken finally looked Will straight in the eye, and he watched as Will's face paled. But the look in his

eyes . . . it wasn't surprise. It was something else—
something that almost looked like *guilt*.

A wave of nausea spread through Ken, and he
sank into the chair next to where he was standing.
The silence between them was absolutely unbearable
as Ken waited for Will to say something. Finally Ken
coughed. "So, uh, I guess you knew she was spreading that rumor around, then, huh?" he asked, wondering if his voice sounded as high-pitched to Will as
it did to him.

Will swallowed. "When did she tell you that?" he
asked. "And what did she say, exactly?"

Ken glanced away, feeling his face heat up. "Maria
and I ran into her at House of Java," he said. "She announced it to us in front of all her friends—how my
dad told Krubowski he could get him a cushy coaching job if I landed the scholarship." He looked back
at Will. "Will, what's going on?" he asked, his tone
low. "Why would Melissa say something so crazy?"

He stared at Will, who opened his mouth and
then closed it again. The guy didn't know what to
say. There was only one reason he would be acting
like this. *Because it's not crazy,* Ken thought, feeling
every one of his internal organs compress until he
could barely breathe.

"It's true—isn't it?" Ken said, the words tasting
bitter as he got them out. Will just shook his head.

CHAPTER 7

Reality Check

Conner wandered up a winding set of stairs that led to—surprise—another bar. This place was loaded with them.

When he'd left the hotel where he, Evan, and Jeremy were staying, he'd walked a few blocks down the strip to try to get a feel for the area. He'd been just about ready to turn around and head back when he saw a sign for a resort that supposedly had a world-famous collection of antique and classic cars. He'd decided to check the place out, but he'd been walking around it for a half hour now and he hadn't found a single car.

Maybe he'd read the sign wrong. *Maybe it was a world-class collection of* bars, he thought as he passed yet another lounge full of people and clanking glasses. It was almost too much to take. If he didn't find what he was looking for soon, he was going to have to retreat to the doo-wop diner and his ever so amusing buddy, Jeremy.

Conner headed back down the staircase, through a narrow hallway, and up another staircase that appeared to lead to a balcony. When he reached the landing at the top, he almost laughed out loud. It was another lounge—only this one was practically deserted. He had started to turn around when someone called out to him.

"Hey—you look like you could use a drink. What'll it be?" Conner scowled and stared at the bartender, a slender, thirtyish woman with long, blond hair pulled back into a ponytail and way too much eye makeup.

He was about to tell her, "Thanks, but no thanks," when a bottle just behind her caught his eye. It was Stolichnaya vodka, and it had been his favorite drink—the one that had been largely responsible for his stint in rehab.

Just looking at the label, he felt like he could taste it—feel the warmth of it sliding down his throat, the way it coated his stomach. He remembered the way after a few drinks rooms always seemed a little darker, more intimate. The way it took the edge off things and even made people like Jeremy—with all their uptight rules and schedules—bearable. He'd give almost anything for that feeling right now— that calm, that ease. That drink.

They'd always made such a big deal in rehab

She groaned. "Don't get sappy on me," she said. "We've still got a lot to see."

"I'm not getting sappy," Evan insisted. "I'm just really glad I bumped into you—otherwise I never would have found any of this stuff. Plus you're really cool." Laney narrowed her eyes and studied his face. "So what's next?" he asked. Then, leaning closer, he added, "Or is that the best you can do?"

"Is that a challenge?" Laney asked, her eyes widening.

"Only if you think you can handle it," Evan responded.

"Viva Las Vegas," Laney declared just as the elevator bell rang. She stepped inside, pulling Evan with her. "We're going to see a show."

"Can I freshen that for you? Again?" Maggie asked, holding the pot of decaf over Jeremy's cold cup.

"Yeah. I guess," Jeremy said, even though his throat was starting to feel a little pasty from all the coffee he'd had that night. "Actually—how about a glass of water?"

"Sure," Maggie said, bouncing back to the kitchen. She was still hustling around, even though Jeremy was virtually the only customer in the diner at the moment. Still, according to Maggie, this was where all the workers from the strip came when they wanted a good cup of coffee—when they got off work, which was, of course, after midnight.

"Here you go," Maggie said, setting down a tall glass with plenty of ice water and a lemon wedge on the side.

"Thanks," Jeremy said, taking a long sip. He couldn't believe neither Conner nor Evan had come back yet. What were they doing? "Uh—Maggie?" he said, realizing how odd it felt to be on a first-name basis with his waitress.

"Mm-hmm?"

"I'm going to run out and use the pay phone again. I'll be right back."

"Okay," she said, calling from the grill out back. Jeremy wasn't sure why he'd told her, except that he would have felt rude if he hadn't. She had, after all, been taking care of him all night—feeding him pie and coffee at no charge, insisting all the while that Laney wouldn't want him to have to pay.

When he reached the phone, he punched in his family's number again, from memory this time. This was the fourth time he'd tried, and he found that he wasn't even expecting an answer anymore.

"Hello?" Mrs. Aames said.

"Mom!" Jeremy cried. "I've been trying you all night—where have you been? Is everyone okay?"

Mrs. Aames laughed on the other end of the

phone. "Of course we're okay—why wouldn't we be?"

"I—I don't know, I just . . . when there wasn't any answer, I—" Jeremy let his voice trail off. Not only did his mother sound fine, she sounded completely unconcerned about him.

"How about you? How's the *road trip* going?" She pronounced the words with a playful lilt in her voice, as if he was on some kind of kooky adventure out of a movie or something.

"It's . . . okay," Jeremy said. Of course what he really wanted to say was that it was horrible. They were off course, Evan and Conner were missing in action, and they were probably going to be late arriving tomorrow, but he didn't want to worry her. Or maybe he did. A *little* concern in her voice would be nice. "Actually, it's not going so well," he added.

"Really? What's wrong? The car's holding up okay, isn't it?"

"Yeah, the car's fine, Mom. I'm sorry, I should have said that," Jeremy apologized. It wasn't like he wanted to upset her. "It's just that . . . well, we're in Vegas."

"Vegas?" his mother echoed. He couldn't tell from her tone just what she thought of that. Then she let out another laugh. "Jeremy, what are you doing in Vegas?" she asked.

"Well, Evan thought it would be a cool place to

stop, so we sort of rearranged our schedule a little," Jeremy explained.

"That's great," Mrs. Aames said. "You deserve a little fun—so are you having a good time? Do you have a room?"

"Yeah, we've got a room."

"Jeremy—what's wrong? You sound upset," his mother said. "You're being responsible, aren't you?" she added, the concern creeping back into her voice. "No drinking?"

Jeremy took a deep breath. "No, Mom, we're just taking in the sights, I promise," he replied. "I just feel bad because I think coming here is going to make us a little late getting to your place tomorrow, and I want to be there to help as soon as I can."

"Oh, Jeremy." His mother sighed. "I appreciate it, really, I do. And we're all very excited to see you— Emma's pretending she doesn't miss you, of course, but at the same time she can't stop talking about you." Jeremy chuckled. "But you've got to stop worrying about us so much. We're doing fine. Your aunt and uncle have been feeding us like crazy, and we all went out to dinner tonight. . . . We're fine. Really. Why don't you just concentrate on having a good time with your friends, and we'll see you when you get here. Okay?"

"Okay," Jeremy said, trying to keep the gloom out of his voice.

"I love you, sweetie."

"I love you too, Mom," Jeremy said, hanging up.

When he was back on his bar stool in the coffee shop, Jeremy thought of everything his mother had said. Why hadn't she been concerned about the fact that he was hundreds of miles off his route? Or that he and his "friends" as she had called them had decided to stop in Las Vegas on a whim? It didn't make sense. Weren't parents *supposed* to worry about those things?

"Coffee?" Maggie offered, the pot hovering over his mug again.

"Yeah," Jeremy said. "But give me the regular." He was going to need some caffeine if he was going to wait up for Conner and Evan. Maybe he didn't need to worry about his family anymore since they were all doing so great without him, but he figured he should at least make sure his roomies made it back to the hotel okay. After all, they were probably expecting him to wait up—weren't they?

One little drink, the voice inside Conner's head seemed to whisper. No, not whisper. Not anymore. It was getting louder and louder, and his feet were taking him closer and closer to the bar, to that beautiful bottle of vodka.

He was almost there when a vision of himself

facedown on the rocks at Crescent Beach, where Evan had found him that time, slammed into his brain and gave him the reality check he needed.

"No, I don't want anything," he finally managed, spitting the words out with such venom that the bartender almost looked like she'd been slapped. Conner shook his head. "Sorry," he muttered. "I just don't want a drink."

She stared at him for a second, then winced. "I think I'm the one who should be apologizing," she said.

Conner blinked. "What?"

She glanced at him again, and he realized that her eyes were filled with pity. "I should have seen it," she said. "I should never have offered you a drink. I'm usually better at spotting . . . well, people who have problems with alcohol."

Conner shifted his weight from one foot to the other and folded his arms across his chest. She was right, of course, but he didn't exactly enjoy being analyzed by a complete stranger—that was Evan's gig.

"Look, I've gotta go," he said. Better to leave now before the bartender with a heart started offering up free psychoanalysis.

"Oh—wait—I didn't mean to upset you," she said. "I know it's none of my business. It's just that, well, my brother's an alcoholic, and he used to get that same glazed look whenever he visited me at work." Conner stopped, keeping his eyes fixed on the floor but not making a move to walk away. "I guess I should say he's a *recovering* alcoholic—he hasn't had a drink in over three years," she continued. "It was really tough at first, but he's doing a lot better with it now. For a long time he couldn't even come here to see me—it was too tempting."

Conner bit his lip. He could understand that all too well.

"Of course, the most important time to steer clear of alcohol altogether is in that first year," she went on, her voice soft. "And anytime you're dealing with a lot of stress—at least that's what my brother says, and I guess he should know." Conner felt himself tense up, and immediately he thought of the way Alanna had looked the other night—the way her breath had smelled of too much mouthwash, like she was trying to hide something. And somehow he knew she was.

"But what if your friends drink?" he heard himself say, even though he hadn't really meant to ask the question out loud.

"Get new friends," the bartender said, leaning forward to wipe down the counter. "Or at least find some that have the decency to support you instead of risking your sobriety. For people like my brother, alcohol is poison. And anyone who doesn't help him stay away is just an enabler."

Enablers. That had been a big word at rehab. Fortunately, none of Conner's friends had played that role—at least not once they realized he had a problem. Instead they'd tried to stop him. But he wasn't sure Alanna would do the same thing. She might even be drinking again already. So did that mean he had to stop hanging out with her the way the bartender's brother had stopped visiting her at work?

Conner sighed. That couldn't be the answer—his situation was different. It wasn't a question of avoiding someone's workplace; it was a question of avoiding the person altogether. And Alanna just happened to be a person he cared about. A lot.

Still, if he stayed with Alanna and if Alanna was drinking again, would he actually be able to help her?

"Look, I know I'm sticking myself into your business when I don't even know you," the bartender said. Conner finally raised his head back up to meet her gaze. "But this place is a major danger zone, and I wouldn't want you to do something you'd regret. So do yourself a favor and get back to your hotel room, okay?" Conner looked back at her awkwardly, then nodded, figuring that's what she was expecting. "And any of those friends you've got, the ones who still drink around you?" she said. "You don't need them. Remember that."

Right. Okay. Just one problem—he did need Alanna. And until this moment he hadn't even realized it or realized how *much* he needed her. But he did, and it was way too late to let go.

Ken Matthews

Dad—

It's ten o'clock, and you're still not home. Where are you? Out having a beer with your good friend Hank Krubowski?

That's right—I found out about the scholarship. Why'd you do it anyway? Did you think I couldn't get it on my own? Did you think I wasn't good enough? Didn't you think I at least deserved a chance to earn it? Or were you just too sick of having a son who's such a loser to wait around anymore?

If that's the case, I've got news for you—I know exactly how you feel.

"I had a great time," Angel said, staring into Tia's eyes.

"Me too," Tia agreed. She was standing on the porch outside her front door, and Angel was standing on the first step, which made them about the same height. It was the way they had always stood to kiss good night back when they were dating, and Tia couldn't help thinking about how amazing Angel's kisses had always been. Especially with his face as close to hers as it was now.

"The movie sucked," Angel said quietly.

"I know." Tia giggled, still holding his gaze. He seemed to be moving closer, but Tia couldn't tell if it was intentional or if he was just swaying.

"You're beautiful," Angel whispered in a voice that was so sweet, Tia felt her heart melt.

"Thank you," she whispered back, her breath catching slightly. And now she knew Angel was moving closer. His face was just inches from hers now— so close, she could feel his breath.

135

"I'm glad we got together," he added, even more quietly.

"Me too," Tia breathed, and when she closed her eyes, Angel pressed his lips to hers, making her shoulders quiver. He deepened the kiss, putting his arms around her and pulling her closer. Tia was shivering with excitement, but at the same time she felt like she could absolutely melt into him. But just when she thought she wanted to throw her arms around him and never let go, Angel pulled back.

"Can I call you tomorrow?" he asked.

"You'd better," Tia managed, even though she was practically out of breath. Angel grinned, then kissed her hand gently and let it drop, turning to walk to his car. Tia watched him all the way down the path—one part of her wanting to run after him and kiss him longer, but a larger part savoring the moment and the way Angel had ended the night so beautifully.

On the one hand, it was like they'd never broken up at all. But at the same time it was so romantic and sweet that it felt like a first date all over again. Tia sighed as he drove away, then stepped inside, a dreamy smile on her face. Her date with Angel had been nothing less than perfect.

She could hardly wait to e-mail Andy and let him know how wrong he'd been.

*   *   *

"So what did you think of the show?" Laney asked as she and Evan sat down for coffee. She'd taken him to a coffee shop that was popular with Las Vegas locals—not tourists—and to Evan's surprise, it actually reminded him of House of Java. Unpretentious, simple wooden tables and chairs and plain old coffee. Very cool, although not very Vegas.

"The show was great," Evan said, referring to the performance of *Viva Las Vegas* Laney had gotten him into—for free. "I just can't believe you actually play Madonna," he said.

"Only Tuesday through Saturday," Laney said with a casual shrug. "Sundays and Mondays, Celine Dion gets center stage."

Evan laughed. "You act like it's no big deal."

"It's a job," Laney said. "A cool job, yeah, but it's not what I see myself doing five years from now."

"What *do* you see yourself doing?" Evan asked, leaning forward across the table.

"I'm not sure," Laney said. "Whatever comes next, I guess. I haven't really figured that out yet."

"Does that bother you?" he asked, raising his eyebrows slightly in surprise.

"What?" she asked.

"The not-knowing thing—it doesn't bug you?"

Laney stared into the distance for a minute, considering it. "Not really."

"Wow—that's amazing." Evan shook his head. "Everyone I know is freaking out right now because we're about to graduate and they all seem to think they need to have the rest of their lives planned out. But here you are, just rolling with it and doing fine. It's . . . well, amazing."

"Yeah, but you make it sound like I don't have any plans at all," Laney pointed out.

"You don't," Evan said.

"No *specific* plans," she said, "but I have direction."

"I don't get it," Evan said. "What's the difference?"

"You don't need a five-year plan to have direction in life," Laney explained. Evan took a sip of his coffee and squinted at her. "Okay, I'll give you an example," she went on. "I've always loved acting."

"That's a shock," Evan joked.

"So," Laney continued, "I went to college and majored in drama with a minor in English. But I don't want to be a movie star. Not many people make it in that business, and the ones that do work long hours and have to worry about security and privacy and stalkers and all that stuff—definitely not my scene. So instead I came here."

"Wait a minute—where are you from?" Evan asked. Somehow he'd just assumed Laney had always lived in Nevada.

"Connecticut," she said.

"You're kidding!"

"Nope. I'm a Yankee, born and bred in New England."

"And you just . . . came to Vegas on a whim?" Evan asked.

"I guess we've got something in common," Laney shot back.

Evan grinned.

"So I'll probably hang out here for a while longer," she continued, "save up some more money, and pretend to be Madonna five nights a week until it gets tired. Then I'll think things over and figure out where to go next."

"Wow," Evan said, in total awe of Laney's free spirit. The girl was incredible—like no one he'd ever met before.

"Of course, I'm pretty sure I want to head back to Connecticut—or at least the East Coast—at some point because that area just feels like home to me, but for now, this is good," Laney said, stirring her coffee. "And I'm putting away enough money that I won't have to worry for a while when I decide to move on."

Evan took a sip of his coffee, then shot another glance at Laney, focusing in on her face. She had the most beautiful green eyes he'd ever seen, with flecks of gold around the pupil, but it wasn't the color or shape that made them stand out. It was the light inside them.

"I know I keep saying this, but I'm so glad I ran into you here," Evan said. "You don't know how great this night has been for me." After being all caught up in the Jessica-Elizabeth-Jade dramas for the last few months, he was finally getting exactly what he needed. A night to just have fun—without worries, without strings, without having to please somebody else.

"I'm having a good time too," Laney said. "You're a fun guy, Evan."

"Thanks," Evan said, his cheeks getting warm. "It's so weird—you know? I just met you tonight, but I feel totally comfortable with you. And I also feel so . . . I don't know—alive, I guess. So . . . free—"

"Well, don't get too used to it," Laney said, standing up. She gulped down her coffee, took Evan by the hand, and began pulling him toward the door.

"Where are we off to now?" he asked, laughing.

Laney turned to him, a mischievous grin spreading across her face. "The wedding chapel, of course."

Jeremy finished the last sips of his mug, then ran his hand lightly over his stomach. The three cups of regular coffee he'd downed in the last hour felt like they were beginning to eat through the lining of his intestines.

"Oh—no more, Maggie, thanks," he said as she

came hustling out of the kitchen with the coffeepot.

"It's not for you," she said, setting the full pot on top of a warmer, "but this is." She unfolded a piece of paper and gave it to him. "Laney called and said you and Conner should leave right away and meet her and Evan at this address. She said they needed a couple of witnesses."

Jeremy shook his head. "Witnesses?" he said, studying the address and glancing up at Maggie. "What is this place?"

"A wedding chapel," Maggie said casually.

Jeremy nearly knocked his mug off the counter. "A what?" he said, standing up. It was as if all the caffeine he'd consumed was kicking in at once.

"A wedding chapel," Maggie repeated.

"Oh my God, I've got to get over there," Jeremy cried. "How do I—?"

"If you need to get there that fast, take a taxi," Maggie interrupted. "It'll be easier."

"Thanks," Jeremy said, slapping a twenty-dollar bill on the counter. It was the least he could do for all the free coffee and snacks. He ran out of the café, turned left and then right, and spotted a line of taxis in front of the next hotel down. Immediately he began running toward them. Was Evan actually taking this whole one-wild-night-to-cut-loose-and-go-crazy thing so far that he'd actually get *married*?

141

As he pulled open one of the taxi doors and hopped in, Jeremy suddenly remembered that Maggie had said he was supposed to bring Conner too. He hesitated, considering getting back out, but where was he supposed to look for Conner? It could take him all night just to find him, and there obviously wasn't time for that now. He had to get to the chapel and stop Evan from making the biggest mistake of his life.

"Nine twenty-two South Main Street," he told the driver, reading straight from the note Maggie had given him. "And I'm in a rush."

"This is it," Laney said as she and Evan hopped out of the cab. "Should we go in?"

"Sure," Evan said, following her up the stairs without question. He didn't know what had come over him, but somehow he wasn't about to stop Laney, whatever she was planning for them. It wasn't clear exactly what Laney had in mind, but Evan knew one thing for certain—this had been the most exciting night of his life, and he wasn't ready for it to end.

"The Elvis Chapel," Laney said as they walked in.

Evan stared around him at all the bright, neon colors. The place was actually much smaller than he would have thought—it looked sort of like the inside of some tacky fast-food restaurant. There were big signs on the wall, listing the names of people who had been married there, and strange glittery decorations around them. "This is cool," he finally said.

"And you're pretty cool too," Laney said, turning to smile at him. "I can't believe you never asked once on the way over why I was bringing you here."

Evan smirked. "I figured you had your reasons," he replied, even though the nerves were actually starting to rev up inside him. His name wasn't going to be added to that list tonight, was it?

"Well, you've been so great about everything, I guess I should probably let you in on the secret now," she said. She paused, taking his hand in hers, her eyes sparkling. "We're not here to get married," she announced, then started to laugh. "But you probably guessed that already," she added.

Evan managed a smile and a quiet laugh, but for some reason he couldn't quite comprehend, his relief was mixed with a little disappointment. It wasn't like he had actually intended to get married, but some crazy instinct in him must have been into the idea of just letting everything go like that.

"So—what, then?" he asked..

"We're going to be *in* someone's wedding," Laney informed him.

Evan scrunched up his nose. "Whose?"

"Whoever," Laney said with a shrug. "We'll just

let the wedding planner know that we want to serve as witnesses, and then we'll wait for the next couple to come in. They don't mind as long as you look semitrustworthy—which means we might need to pat down that hair of yours," she said. She laughed again, then reached up to press her hand to his head. "And it's fun—we get to watch an unusual wedding and sign the marriage license."

Evan shook his head. "And let me guess—Elvis is the justice of the peace?"

"You got it!" Laney answered. "You know, you ought to think of moving to Vegas—you'd do well here," she told him, which only made Evan laugh more. "Oh—and I forgot to tell you," Laney continued. "I called the diner at your hotel and left Jeremy and Conner a message to meet us here—I thought they might enjoy this too, from everything you've told me about them."

Evan smiled. "Yeah, definitely," he agreed. "But wait—did you make it clear *why* they were supposed to meet us here?"

Laney bit her lip. "Not *exactly*," she said. "I mean, when you only have one night in Vegas, you have to make it a night you'll never forget," she explained.

Evan threw back his head and laughed. He could hardly wait to see the looks on Conner and Jeremy's faces when they got here, probably in a complete panic. This night just kept getting better and better.

To: mfox@swiftnet.com
From: wsimmons@swiftnet.com
Subject: Secret?

Melissa,
   We need to talk. I just saw Ken at
his dad's office and he was a mess.
What were you thinking, telling him
about the scholarship?
   I'm beginning to realize that I
can't trust you with anything.
                    —Will

<DELETE MESSAGE>

To: mfox@swiftnet.com
From: wsimmons@swiftnet.com
Subject: Secret?

Melissa,
  We need to talk.

                    —Will

            <SEND MESSAGE>

CHAPTER
Sure Thing
9

"You're late," Ken said when his father walked into the kitchen that night, seconds after Ken had heard the front door open and close. Ken was sitting at the kitchen table with the lights out, where he'd been for he didn't even know how long—just waiting.

"Ken," Mr. Matthews said. "What are you doing sitting here in the dark?" He reached over and flicked on the light, causing Ken to squint.

"Thinking," Ken replied. It was the truth, partly.

"About anything in particular?" Mr. Matthews ventured. But he didn't really sound interested. More like irritated that Ken was wasting his time.

"About the scholarship you bought me," Ken said, his voice filled with bitterness.

There was a long pause. Extremely long. Was it morning yet?

"What are you talking about?" Mr. Matthews said, his whole face tight.

"Don't bother," Ken said. "I know what you did."

Mr. Matthews nodded. "Okay, then," he said. "How'd you find out?"

Ken felt his jaw drop open. Yeah, he'd told his dad not to act dumb. But he'd still been waiting for the denial to come—and hoping too, he realized with a sick feeling. He'd been hoping deep down that this was all a lie or a misunderstanding or something. That somehow his dad would explain it all, and Ken would know that he'd earned that scholarship himself.

"What—you're not even going to deny it?" Ken spat out, bile rising up in his throat. "Or, I don't know . . . *apologize?*"

"Why should I apologize?" Mr. Matthews asked, looking genuinely confused. He slid into the seat opposite Ken. "I did this for you, son."

"That's the problem!" Ken yelled. "You did it *for* me. Did you ever stop to think that maybe I could do it myself?"

"Of course I did," Mr. Matthews said smoothly. Ken threw his hands up in the air, barely able to listen to another of his father's lines. "But I just thought it would be better if I could make it a sure thing," he added.

"Dad—you *bribed* Hank Krubowski. Don't you think there's something *wrong* about that?" Ken demanded.

"Actually, no—I don't," his father replied. "People do this kind of thing all the time. It's the way the world works, Ken. A good percentage of the people that go to schools like Harvard and Yale get in because they know someone—not because of their grades. This isn't any different. I knew someone who could help Hank, so Hank helped me. What's so bad about that?"

"*Hank?*" Ken repeated with disgust. "What—you're on a first-name basis with him now?"

"He's a good man," Mr. Matthews said.

"*What?*" Ken felt ready to explode. "You *bribed* someone to get me that scholarship, and now there's no way I can even go to Michigan. It's too expensive without the scholarship, and you've ruined my chances to get it."

"What do you mean, 'ruined your chances'? You've *got* it. I don't understand why you aren't thanking me."

Ken's breath came in short gasps as he struggled to remain in control. "But I can't accept it," he said, shaking his head back and forth, back and forth. "Not like this."

"Why not?" his father asked.

"Because it's—it's *wrong.*"

Mr. Matthews sighed. "Right and wrong are relative terms, Ken. You'll learn that when you get out in the world and start making your own decisions. But for right now, the way I see it, I'm still waiting for my thanks. A lot of guys your age would be thrilled to have fathers who could open doors like this for them."

"You don't get it," Ken nearly whispered, all the energy drained from him. "You don't get anything that doesn't have a scoreboard. I could have won that scholarship—I know I could have. You haven't given me a chance—you've taken one away."

Mr. Matthews shrugged. "Look at it however you want," he said, "but just don't go throwing away an opportunity like this because you're a little upset. You're *in*, Ken. You don't have to worry anymore, you don't have to scrounge for student loans, and you don't have to fill out any more college applications. You're all set."

Ken buried his head in his hands and groaned in frustration.

"Seriously, Ken," his father continued. "You're already a Wolverine—you don't even have to try out for the team. Are you really going to give all that up just because it didn't happen the way you wanted it to?" Then Mr. Matthews flicked out the light and walked upstairs to his bedroom, leaving Ken alone in the darkness. Again.

"Thanks," Jeremy said as the cab came to a halt outside a white building with a flowery sign that read, The Elvis Chapel. He handed the driver a ten-dollar bill and sprang out of the cab without even waiting for his change—there was no time to waste.

He grabbed the black wrought-iron handrail and took the concrete steps two at a time. When he threw open the tall, narrow door at the top and plunged through it, he found himself in a bench-lined waiting room with floral wallpaper and a bright green carpet, but there was no sign of Evan or Laney.

"Can I help you?" asked an older woman who was sitting behind a rounded desk in the corner, staring at him over her spectacles.

"Yeah," Jeremy said breathlessly, his chest pounding. "I'm looking for two friends—a guy and a girl."

"We get a lot of couples." The lady nodded, giving him a grandmotherly smile.

"Oh. Yeah. I guess you would," Jeremy said, his eyes darting around the room for some clue as to where they might be. There were two sets of doors on the far wall, one of which was painted blue, the other pink. The pink one was marked, Do Not Enter. Service in Progress.

Suddenly Jeremy heard organ music beginning, and his heart lurched. "Oh, no—I've got to stop them," he cried. He lunged toward the pink double doors, but the old woman grabbed his arm.

"You can't go in there," she told him, but Jeremy

knew he had to. He broke free from her grasp and was just about to fling open the door when he heard someone call his name.

"Jeremy—we were beginning to think you'd gotten lost," Laney said, exiting the blue room with Evan close behind her. Jeremy released the doorknob to the pink room and rushed toward them.

"Is this boy a friend of yours, Evan?" the old woman asked, her brow creased with concern.

"Oh, yeah, thanks, Evelyn," Evan said, nodding. "He's okay." The old woman—or *Evelyn*—walked back to her desk just as Jeremy grabbed Evan's hand.

"Am I too late?" he asked, scanning his friend's fingers. "Oh, man, no ring," he breathed, letting Evan's hand drop and heaving a huge sigh of relief.

"You don't need a ring to get married," Laney said casually.

"It's just a symbol," Evan agreed. "It doesn't have any legal purpose. Personally, I've never wanted one."

"Me neither," Laney agreed with a shrug. Then she took Evan's hand in hers and stared into his eyes. "We have so much in common," she said, smiling up at him.

The room seemed to blur at the edges, and Jeremy's head felt like it was spinning. "No—you didn't. . . . You couldn't have." He stared at Evan in disbelief, shaking his head and wondering how a simple road trip to Arizona could have gone so terribly wrong.

"But we did," Evan said. "And we need to go back into the chapel for the next one too."

"The next one?" Jeremy wheezed. "What do you mean?" He darted his eyes from Evan to Laney and back again, waiting for some kind of explanation, but they just stared. Then, after what seemed like an eternity of silence to Jeremy, they both burst out laughing.

"What? What's going on?" Jeremy asked, still frantic. How either of them could find this situation even remotely funny was beyond him.

"Oh, Jeremy—I'm sorry," Evan said, slapping him on the back. "We're not married. We were just having a little fun with you."

"W-What?" Jeremy asked. "You mean . . . this is just . . . a joke?" Evan and Laney grinned, but Jeremy still wasn't laughing. Didn't they realize what they had just put him through?

"I don't believe this," he said, glaring at them. "You made me rush all the way out here in the middle of the night, thinking you were about to make the biggest mistake of your life," he continued, pointing at Evan, "just for your own amusement?"

"Hey! I resent that," Laney said, narrowing her eyes. "Evan might be a little young to get married, but marrying *me* certainly wouldn't be the biggest mistake of his life."

Jeremy shook his head and threw his hands up in the air. "I don't believe this," he said again. "How can you be so—"

"Hey, Jer—shhh," Evan interrupted, putting a finger to his lips. The organ music had stopped, and for some reason Evan had decided they all needed to whisper now. "We didn't get you all the way out here just to play a joke on you, man. We just thought you might need a little fun."

"A little fun?" Jeremy sneered, not bothering to lower his voice at all. "I—"

"Shhh!" Laney hissed. "Ariel and Jimmy are about to start their service."

Ariel and Jimmy? Jeremy thought, curling his lip. This was getting way too weird.

"Seriously, man," Evan whispered, "I'm sorry if we freaked you out, but—just come on." He jerked his head toward the pink door as if he actually expected Jeremy to go in. When Jeremy didn't move, Evan grabbed him by the elbow and started to guide him. Jeremy dug in his heels and tried to resist, but Evan was stronger than he'd thought. "We weren't joking when we said we have to get back in there," Evan continued quietly. "We're the witnesses for this next wedding."

"Witnesses?"

"Yeah," Laney said. "You can be one too. It'll be fun."

"I don't—" Jeremy began to protest, but Evan had already opened the door to the chapel and pushed him through. The couple at the altar turned to stare at him—sending him into sufficient shock to render him speechless. The bride—who was about six-two—stood straight in her lime green chiffon dress, and the groom—who couldn't have been many inches over five feet—had his head bent down. He was wearing a powder blue tux, like something out of a bad movie from decades ago. Jeremy stopped dead in his tracks, then let Evan push him down the aisle and into the first pew.

What am I doing here? Jeremy wondered, looking around the room. The same bright green carpet that blanketed the waiting area covered the chapel floor as well. But instead of the pink floral wallpaper the chapel walls were an off-white and were adorned with huge pictures of Elvis painted on velvet and cut and framed to look like stained-glass windows.

The altar, where the couple stood, included a white garden trellis covered in sparkly, blue roses and green vines and a gold-lettered sign that read, What the King Has Joined Together, Let No Man Put Asunder. Jeremy rubbed his temples, barely able to believe what he was seeing, and he was just about convinced that things couldn't get any more bizarre when his eyes landed on the man who stood in front of the couple. It was Elvis. Or at least an Elvis impersonator, and a pretty good one at that.

Jeremy immediately recognized the black leather pants, jacket, and boots he was wearing as perfect reproductions of the ones Elvis wore on the '68 *Comeback Special* tape that Mrs. Aames liked to watch every once in a while. He even had a red scarf tied around his neck—just like Elvis had—and when he spoke, Jeremy could have sworn he was looking at the real thing.

"Ladies and gentlemen, I wanna thank ya— thank ya very much for comin' together today to witness the joinin' of Ariel and Jimmy."

Jeremy blinked rapidly and cupped his hand to his mouth. Apparently he had laughed too, though he wasn't aware of it until Laney smacked his stomach lightly with the back of her hand. "Sorry," Jeremy said, clearing his throat and chuckling again in spite of himself.

Laney and Evan both turned to him this time. They were smiling but at the same time imploring him with their eyes to keep quiet. Jeremy nodded and coughed a few times, trying to maintain his composure, but he couldn't keep the laughter from swelling inside his chest. It was all just so absurd!

He glanced over at the couple again and tried to pull it together for their sake, but his entire body had begun to shake with silent laughter now, and tears were welling up in the corners of his eyes.

"Jeremy," Evan whispered, but all Jeremy could do was shake his head. And then he exploded.

Jeremy doubled over, his laughter ringing out through the chapel. "I'm sorry," he rasped every time he could manage enough breath to speak. When finally he managed to regain enough control that he could actually wipe the moisture away from his eyes and look up, everyone—Laney, Evan, Ariel, Jimmy, the organ player, and even Elvis—was staring at him.

"Oh," Jeremy said, taking a deep breath. "Excuse me. Please. I'm really sorry. You can . . . you can go on now. I'll, uh, just wait outside," he added, but as he started to make his way past Laney and Evan, the bride stopped him.

"Aw, shoot, sugar," she drawled in the thickest southern accent Jeremy had ever heard up close and personal. "Don't leave now—you were just startin' to enjoy yourself." Jeremy gazed into her eyes—once he found them below all the blue eye shadow—and was shocked to see that she was actually smiling at him.

"Uh—are you sure?" he asked.

"Son," Elvis chimed in. "There are two things you need to understand about the Chapel of Elvis: first, we don't mind a little laughter, and second—no one leaves until I'm done singing." Then he flipped a switch on his lectern, filling the chapel with soft guitar music, and grabbed a microphone. *"Love me tender, love me dear,"* he began as Jeremy walked back to his place.

Jeremy's heart was still beating a little fast from everything he'd just been through—especially his laughing fit—but to his surprise, he felt more relaxed, more at ease, and more lighthearted than he had for a while. He grinned when the Elvis impersonator winked at him, realizing for the first time something that Elvis had apparently known all along—everyone could use a good laugh.

"This is it, right here," Laney told the cabdriver as he pulled up in front of the hotel where Evan, Conner, and Jeremy were staying. Evan reached for his wallet, but Laney held up her hand. "I've got it," she said, handing the driver a few bills.

"You don't have to—"

"Don't argue," Laney told him, opening her door and getting out. Evan and Jeremy both slid out after her. "You've still got a lot of days left in your road trip—buy yourself a souvenir."

Evan chuckled. "I don't think I'm going to need one to remember this trip."

"And hey, we already have one," Jeremy said, pulling a red scarf from his jacket pocket.

"Jeremy!" Laney squealed. "That's Elvis's scarf!"

Jeremy laughed and nodded. "I know. I told him how much my mom loved his comeback special and he gave it to me."

"Way to go, man!" Evan said, slapping him a high five. Jeremy had really loosened up after his giggle fit in the chapel—he and Evan had even sung backup for Elvis when he did "Teddy Bear" later in the ceremony. And Laney had gotten the photographer to take a picture of the three of them with Elvis, which she promised to get copies of and mail to Evan when they came in.

"Well—it's getting late," Laney said. "I've got to get home and rest up—Madonna's back onstage tomorrow night."

Evan gazed into her eyes and smiled. He knew it was time to say good-bye, no matter how much he wished this night could go on forever. "I don't know how to thank you," he told her, shaking his head. "I had such an amazing time."

Laney took his hands in hers and returned the smile. "You don't need to thank me," she said. "I had a great time too. You let me do a lot of stuff through a fresh pair of eyes tonight, and it was nice. And Jeremy," Laney called, breaking away from Evan suddenly. "You keep smiling!"

"I will," Jeremy said with a nod.

Laney turned back to Evan and sighed. "Okay. I hate good-byes, so I'm not even going to say it.

Here's my address and phone number in case you're on your way through again anytime soon," she said, passing him a scrap of paper on which she'd scribbled all the information, "and if you feel like writing, let me know how the rest of your senior year goes and what you decide to do next."

"Will do," Evan said, folding the paper carefully and stuffing it into his wallet. "So—"

"Don't say it," Laney interrupted, holding up one hand.

Evan chuckled. "Okay, I won't. Just . . . take care."

Laney nodded. "I'll see you later," she said. "And you too, Jeremy."

"See ya later, Laney," Jeremy said. Then Laney turned and started down the strip. Evan and Jeremy watched her for a bit, but she never looked back, so eventually they turned and started into the hotel.

"Are you guys just getting back too?"

Evan glanced over and saw Conner walking up from the other direction. "Hey—Conner, man. Where have you been?" Evan asked, slapping his friend on the back.

"Just looking around," Conner said, gazing out at all the lights—none of which had been put out, despite the fact that it was now two o'clock in the morning. "This place is crazy," he added.

"You're not kidding," Evan agreed. "Crazy . . . and amazing."

Jeremy nodded. "Yeah. I'm glad we came." Evan and Conner looked at each other in disbelief, then turned to Jeremy. "What?" Jeremy asked. "I am." He was silent for a moment, then all three of them laughed.

"Hey," Conner said, nodding toward the check-in desk as they passed it. "You want me to check and see if we can get a wake-up call so we can get up early and be in Tucson as soon as possible?"

"A wake-up call?" Jeremy repeated. "No way. After today I'm going to need some serious rest."

Evan's eyebrows shot up in surprise, and he saw Conner's eyes widen as well. So Mr. Man with a Plan was finally relaxing?

"I don't want to get up tomorrow until I'm good and ready," Jeremy added. "After all—this is a *road trip*."

To: wsimmons@swiftnet.com
From: mfox@swiftnet.com

Will—

   I have some bad news. Ken found out
about how his dad bribed the U.
Michigan scout to get him that
scholarship. I tried to keep it from
him—honestly—but he came up to me at
House of Java and started asking all
kinds of questions. I guess he
overheard his dad talking to that guy
about his coaching position on the
phone and got suspicious. He kept
insisting since you work for his dad,
you must know what really happened.
And I guess he figured that if you
had heard anything, you would have
told me.

   I'm really sorry, Will. There
wasn't much I could do.

                         Love,
                         Melissa

Hey, Tia,

So . . . how's everything going
with your break? The football clinic
was great yesterday. The kids are
really funny, and I think one of them
actually learned something from me.
Pretty crazy.

Do you want to try and get
together, like we talked about? Maybe
tonight or tomorrow night?

CHAPTER
DIFFERENT PLACES
10

"Is it scary without your mom and dad around?"
Tomás asked, his almond-shaped eyes widening as
he cuddled into Angel's arms.

Miguel laughed. "You're such a baby, Tomás," he
teased, and of course Jesse joined right in.

"Is it scary?" Jesse repeated in a mocking tone.
"What a stupid question."

"It's not a stupid question at all," Angel assured
Tomás, and immediately the other two stopped teasing. All three of them idolized Angel—they had ever
since Tia had started dating him her freshman year
of high school.

"Actually, it is kind of scary," Angel continued.
"For the first time I have to make all my own decisions, and sometimes that's really hard to do. It's a lot
easier to let your parents figure stuff out for you—so
yeah, I'd say it's a little scary without them around."

"I'm never going to leave home," Tomás said, and
this time even Angel chuckled.

"Well, we'll see how you feel about that in another ten years—okay, Tomás?"

"Okay."

Tia had been sitting on the sofa for the last half hour while Angel fielded questions about college from her brothers—and she had actually learned a few things too. Like that Angel had joined a service fraternity and that he was considering spending his sophomore fall semester in England. She never would have expected him to be interested in either of those things before, but then, he'd been gone for three months. Some things were bound to change. What was important was that their feelings for each other hadn't.

Tia watched as her brothers all piled on top of Angel, realizing that the question-and-answer session had now officially turned into a wrestling match. "Okay, okay," Tia said. "Aren't you guys supposed to be helping out at the deli?"

"No," Jesse yelled as Angel flipped him over and pinned him on the ground.

"Dad gave us the day off," Miguel added.

Tia sighed. "Well, you need to go find something else to do anyway—I want to spend some time with Angel too."

"You can have him tomorrow," Tomás said with a giggle as Angel tickled him fiercely, but Tia had waited long enough.

"Sorry, time's up," she said, stepping in and peeling all three of her brothers away from him. Then, when she had freed Angel from the bottom of the pile, she held out her hand and helped him up. "Want to take a walk?" she asked.

"Sure. I'll catch you guys later," Angel said, and Tia led him to the backyard. They held hands and walked over to the wooden swing set that had been in the same spot for close to ten years now—the Ramirezes had gotten it when Tia was just seven.

"This is still one of my favorite hangouts," Angel said, sitting down on one of the swings.

"Yeah. I still come out here at night sometimes to think," Tia said. She took the swing next to Angel and pushed off gently, gliding over the dirt where the grass had been worn away. "Hey." Angel turned his head toward hers. "I didn't know you'd joined a fraternity. I thought you always said that putting that much testosterone together in one house was just asking for trouble."

Angel laughed. "Did I say that?" he joked, obviously remembering the remark. "Yeah, well, I guess I changed my mind. It's actually a lot of fun hanging out at the frat house. Plus it is a *service* fraternity, so we do a lot of volunteer work and fund-raisers. You know I've always been into community service."

"Yeah, that's true," Tia agreed. Still, it seemed

strange that he never even mentioned it to her in his e-mails. It seemed like a pretty big thing.

"You know what else I've started doing?" Angel asked.

Tia frowned. "What?"

"Boxing."

"Boxing?" Tia echoed, her mouth dropping open. "You're kidding."

"Nope," Angel said. "I go down to the gym twice a week to work out, and then there's sparring on Thursday nights."

"You actually *hit* other people?" Tia asked.

"We wear gear—you know, the big gloves, helmets, mouth guards."

"Still," Tia said, scrunching up her face. "Doesn't it hurt?"

"A little." Angel shrugged.

"So why do you do it? It seems so . . . brutal or barbaric or whatever—two guys getting into a ring and trying to kill each other. Where's the fun in that?"

"We don't try to kill each other, Tia," Angel said. He was beginning to sound a little irritated. "That's not what it's about."

"What is it about?" Tia asked. She couldn't believe that Angel, who had always been so peaceful, could actually be involved in something like boxing.

"It's about strategy—getting more points, using

better moves. And it's a great workout. None of us are trying to hurt each other—we're actually all pretty good friends."

"Really? You mean, you go in there and beat each other up, and then you all go out for coffee or something?"

"Kind of," Angel said. "Look—why don't we talk about something else. What's up with you?"

"Well," Tia said, going through the events of the past few months in her head. "You know about cheering and everything with Conner . . . and I told you about that scholarship I was up for. Oh, I know—volleyball should be starting pretty soon, and it looks like we've got a pretty good team this year. And there's another play in the spring that I'm planning to try out for . . . and oh, yeah—I'm on the prom committee, so that's going to be really cool too. We haven't settled on a theme yet, but I know exactly what I want for a dress—I could even tell you the color now so that you match it—"

"Whoa—hold on, Tia," Angel interrupted. "Don't get too carried away."

"What do you mean?" Tia asked, planting her feet firmly on the ground to stop her swing.

"Just that . . . well, I'd love to go to the prom with you, but I'm not going to be around."

"Why not? It's always the third week in May—you should be done by then."

"Yeah, but I've already signed up for May term."

"May term?" Tia asked.

"It's an extra three weeks of classes after the regular year ends, and I've already signed up for a French language-immersion program."

"Oh," Tia said. She squinted at the grass, another thought suddenly occurring to her. "You won't be able to come see my play either, will you?"

"Probably not," Angel admitted. "My weekends are pretty busy with all the fraternity stuff. It's not so easy for me to get home anymore."

"Oh, boy," Tia said with a weak laugh. She rested her elbows on her knees and cradled her head in her hands. "I just remembered something."

"What's that?" Angel asked. His voice was soft, and he was leaning close to her with sad eyes, as if he knew what she was about to say.

"The reason we broke up," Tia said quietly.

Angel nodded and put his arm around her. "Yeah. Me too." They sat together on the swing set for a few minutes before Tia spoke.

"It's not going to work, is it?" she said.

"I don't think so," Angel agreed. "But not because I don't love you."

"And not because I don't love you," Tia replied, tears collecting in her eyes.

"We're just in different places now," Angel said.

Tia nodded. "It still hurts," she said, leaning into him.

"I know," he said, tightening the circle of his arms around her. "But it won't. Not for too long. And at least we figured it out now instead of a few weeks or even months from now."

"Yeah," Tia agreed, wiping away a tear that had slipped down her cheek. She sniffled and sat up straight. "And at least we're doing this in a better way this time," she added.

"Definitely." Angel chuckled. They stood from the swing set and walked slowly back toward the house.

"You know," Tia said as they approached the sliding-glass door that led into the kitchen. "Even if we're not going to be dating, you're still welcome at casa Ramirez anytime. My brothers and my parents are always happy to see you. And so am I."

"Thanks," Angel said. "I'll keep that in mind."

Tia realized he'd probably be steering clear of her for the rest of this break at least, and maybe even the next, which was probably for the best. For both of them. But there was always summer—after May term, of course. And somehow she knew that even though it might take a little time, eventually they'd be able to hang out again. As friends.

* * *

sound on the plush carpet, and sat down gently on the bed next to Tia.

"Are you all right?" she asked, brushing Tia's hair back away from her face.

"Yeah," Tia said, exhaling heavily. "I guess you saw Angel leave last night."

Mrs. Ramirez nodded. "Yes. And from the look on his face, I could tell he wasn't coming back. Do you want to talk about it?" Tia sat up and swung her legs over the side of the bed, letting them dangle next to her mother's.

"There's actually not a lot to say. I guess we just realized that there was a reason we broke up last time and that it was still there."

Her mother sighed. "Long-distance relationships are hard," she agreed. She put her arm around Tia, and Tia rested her head on her mother's shoulder. "Do you want me to make you some more *huevos rancheros?*" Mrs. Ramirez offered.

Tia giggled. "Like I'd ever say no," she answered, smiling up at her mother. "But you know what? You don't really have to. I mean—you can—I'm not telling you not to," Tia backtracked quickly, causing her mother to laugh. She had no intention of talking her mother out of preparing her favorite meal. "But I'm actually not as sad as I thought I was going to be."

"Really?"

"Yeah, it's kind of weird," Tia said, "but I've been lying here thinking for a while, and I actually feel kind of . . . *relieved*."

"Hmmm. Why do you think that is?" Mrs. Ramirez asked.

Tia pressed her lips together, thinking. "Maybe because even though Angel and I broke up before," she began, "I never really felt like we were finished. It didn't seem *over* to me before, not deep down. But now it does."

"Well, that's good—I guess," her mother said, sounding more like she was asking a question than making a statement.

"Yeah, I think it is," Tia said, nodding. "Because before, it was like I was stuck in limbo. I wasn't seeing Angel, but I wasn't ready to see anybody else either."

"And now you are?"

"I think so," Tia said, smiling up at her mother. Mrs. Ramirez smiled back.

"That reminds me," she said, pulling a piece of paper out of her front jeans pocket. "Andy called."

"He did? When?"

"While Angel was here," her mother replied.

"Oh, no," Tia groaned. "He's going to gloat about this for weeks."

"I don't think so," Mrs. Ramirez said.

"No? Why not?" Tia asked with a frown.

"Because—he told me he hoped you didn't get hurt, but that if things didn't seem to be going well with Angel, I should give you this." She passed the scrap of paper to Tia, who immediately grinned. It was Trent's phone number. She must have left it at Andy's house.

"What a jerk," Tia said, but she couldn't help giggling. She threw her arms around her mother's neck and gave her a peck on the cheek.

"Thanks, Mom," she said, smiling as she bounced out of the room. Thankfully, neither Jesse nor Miguel was tying up the line, talking to one of their five thousand girlfriends. She grabbed the phone and quickly dialed the number, remembering that she'd never answered Trent's e-mail from this morning.

"Hello?" It was Trent.

"Um—hi, Trent. This is Tia."

"Oh, hey," he said. Was she crazy, or could she *hear* him smiling on the other end?

Tia cleared her throat. "So, I was wondering if you still wanted to get together." Her heart sped up with each word she spoke because even though Trent had made the offer earlier, there was still the possibility that he was going to say no, after the way she'd sort of been brushing him off.

"Yeah, sure," he said. "That would be great. Should I pick you up, or do you want to meet somewhere?"

"Unfortunately, I'm vehicularly challenged," Tia said. "So unless you want to meet somewhere within walking distance of my house, I'm going to have to bum a ride."

"No problem," Trent said. "Are you free in fifteen minutes?"

"Um—yeah," Tia said, glancing down at her grungy sweatpants in a panic.

"Okay, I'll see you then."

"All right," Tia agreed, hanging up the phone.

There, she thought, walking back to her room, *that wasn't so hard.* Sure, her blood pressure had risen dangerously high, and her palms were already sweaty at the thought of going out with Trent alone—without her friends there to act as a buffer— but overall, moving on was easy.

Getting ready for a first date with a really cute guy in fifteen minutes, on the other hand . . . *that* was going to be a challenge.

JEREMY AAMES

6:30 P.M.

So, the rest of the ride out to Tucson was cool, and I have to admit, it was kind of nice not to be on such a tight schedule. Besides, we still made pretty good time. Actually, we made better time on the second half of the trip without me holding everyone to a minute-by-minute itinerary— and it was a lot more relaxing too.

The first thing I did when we got to my family's house was give my mom the red scarf. She was so psyched that she searched through box after box until she found her video of the <u>Comeback Special</u> and then made everyone sit down and watch it during dinner. Evan loved it—and my mom loved Evan, which Conner said was no big surprise. He said everyone's mom loves Evan.

But the point is, she really loved the red scarf, and I never would have been able to give it to her if I hadn't been forced to loosen up and let myself off the hook for a while. I wouldn't have thought I'd say this, but I really owe Conner and Evan.

EVAN PLUMMER

7:08 P.M.

I knew this road trip was exactly what I needed, and after the most incredible night of my life with the most incredible girl I've ever met, I'm finally ready to jump back into my life without overthinking everything. I'm just going to follow Laney's lead and go with the flow. And I can't wait to see what comes next.

This is what it comes down to—I have to get Alanna to quit drinking. It's that simple.

Okay, so I can't <u>make</u> her stop any more than my friends were able to make me stop—but that doesn't mean I have to give up without a fight.

ELIZABETH WAKEFIELD

8:32 P.M.

Jess and I talked with our cousin
Becky today, and I was really surprised.
She used to be a total flake, but now
it's like she's pulled her whole life
together. She's already been accepted
to UCLA, and she's even visited the
campus twice to register for some kind
of summer Outward Bound program. Plus
she's planning to spend her junior year
abroad, and she's got a great job lined
up for spring and summer so she can
start saving money for all of it now.

It's so weird. Whenever we used to
get the family together for stuff like
this, people used to rag on Becky and
encourage her to be more responsible—
more like me! But now it's like I'm the
flake. Even Jessica seems to have a

better idea of what she's doing than I do.

So, as soon as we get back from this trip, I'm going to start getting my life back on track. Because if I don't, two years from now when we do this family-reunion thing again, everyone's going to be telling me I should be more like Becky, and I'm not sure I could deal with that.

Check out the **all-new....**

Sweet Valley Web site—

www.sweetvalley.com

New Features

Cool Prizes

The **ONLY** official Web site!

Hot Links

And much more!